I0657240

Shattered Dreams

Naomi Bloom Detective Collection, Volume 2

Sybil H. Taylor

Published by Scripted Publishing House, LLC, 2025.

This is a work of fiction. Similarities to real people, places, or events are entirely coincidental.

SHATTERED DREAMS

First edition. March 15, 2025.

ISBN: 979-8992606805

Written by Sybil H. Taylor.

Special thanks to my husband Robert and daughters Nandi, Anaya, Riana, niece Heather, and Son-Son Jaylen for always supporting me and my business ventures.

In memory of those we have lost, you are forever in our hearts.

Publisher: Scripted Publishing House
    scripted.publishinghouse@gmail.com
    Cover Design by: Kahunart.com
    Interior Formatting by: Sybil H. Taylor

For information regarding permission, write to:
    Scripted Publishing House
    scripted.publishinghouse@gmail.com

About the author

Born and raised in New Orleans, LA, Dr. Sybil H. Taylor is a wife, mother of three daughters, clinical pharmacist, author, and entrepreneur. Dr. Taylor earned a Bachelor of Science degree in pharmacy and a Doctorate in clinical pharmacy. Dr. Taylor has worked in various pharmacy settings, including retail, institutional hospital, and federal government. Dr. Taylor's first novel is Friendly Betrayal. Dr. Taylor has since relocated to Atlanta, Georgia, raised her children and started her own natural skincare business, Scripted Naturals in February 2020.

Acknowledgements

Special thanks to my husband Robert and daughters Nandi, Anaya, Riana, niece Heather, and Son-Son Jaylen for always supporting me and my business ventures.

SYBIL H. TAYLOR

In memory of those we have lost, you are forever in our hearts.

Chapter 1

He spotted Sebastian in the hotel lobby and followed him back to his room. They were far from strangers, so Sebastian did not hesitate to let the man enter the hotel room. The air was thick with tension as the two men stood face to face in the hotel room registered under the name Sebastian Daniels, the setting sun cast long shadows that merged with the darkness of his intention. His jaw was determined, his eyes narrowed to slits as he sized up Sebastian, who returned the gaze with equal ferocity. The silence was deafening, broken only by the distant hum of the city below and the occasional muffled voices from the adjacent rooms, until one of them spoke.

"What the hell are you doing here? You tried to undermine me and warn her?" He hissed with a furrowed brow, his jaw clenched, and a tense posture. His eyes narrowed and his breathing was shallow and rapid.

"Listen to me," Sebastian started.

"I can't believe you'd go behind my back like this. After all I have done for you! You planned to tell her?" he asked angrily.

"I won't be responsible for tearing a family apart and you of all people should agree with me," Sebastian said.

"I am warning you to leave it alone," the man snarled.

"You're trying to ruin her life, you know that, right?" Sebastain said.

"That's not my problem!" The man said.

"This has gone too far, it's time to stop," Sebastian warned, becoming upset.

"And who is going to stop me?" He snapped back ignoring his words.

"Me! She has a young son. Remember how that feels," Sebastian said, trying to reason with him.

Without warning, the man lunged forward, his fist aimed at Sebastian's face. But Sebastian was quick, sidestepping the blow, feeling the rush of air as his fist whizzed past. The fight had begun. They were a cyclone of motion, a dance of destruction. The carpet, once a pattern of vibrant blues and golds, was now just a blur beneath their shuffling feet. Punches were thrown, some finding their mark, others grazing the air.

The sound of flesh hitting flesh echoed off the walls, a testament to the brutality of their encounter. Sebastain ducked as the man swung a lamp at him, its base shattering against the wall where his head had been moments before. Glass rained down, dropping like sharp deadly confetti. Sebastain looked at the wall in shock. And as Sebastian briefly glanced away, the man seized the moment, his fist connecting with Sebastain's stomach, eliciting a painful grunt from him.

The room was in disarray, a chair overturned, the bed sheets torn from the mattress in the scuffle. They were both breathing heavily now, the initial surge of adrenaline giving way to the scrambling burn of fatigue. In a desperate attempt to defend himself, Sebastian grabbed a shard of shattered glass, its jagged edge catching the light. His attacker's eyes widened, but he was ready. With a swift kick, he knocked the shard from Sebastian's hand, sending it skittering across the floor.

The fight moved to the bathroom, the tiles were cold and slippery beneath their feet. Sebastian's back hit the mirror, cracking it, his reflection now as fractured as his resolve. With a last effort to subdue Sebastian, the man grabbed a piece of glass and stabbed Sebastian multiple times as rage coursed through him. Then he pinned Sebastian to the ground, his arm pressed against his throat.

"It's over," he breathed hatefully in Sebastian's ear, his voice steady despite the chaos.

Sebastian's struggle ceased, his body went limp as it conceded defeat. The man stood up slowly over Sebastian, his chest heaving, looking down at the lifeless body who had once been so close to him. The man caught his distorted reflection in a piece of bloody glass. The room was silent once more, the battle concluded. But the fight was far from over. He had to think fast and get out of town. He staged the hotel room to make it appear like an intruder attacked Sebastian. He removed an unmarked envelope of money from Sebastian's pocket, removed the money, and dropped the empty envelope on the floor along with a single hundred-dollar bill.

For a moment a wave of remorse came over him as he looked back at the chaotic scene he was leaving behind. He would now have to alter his plans, but no one could know what happened tonight. The man placed the do not disturb tag on the doorknob as he exited, shutting the door behind him.

The housekeeper, shuffled down the dimly lit corridor, her small hands gripping the cleaning cart. She'd seen it all—the spilled champagne, the forgotten lingerie, the whispered secrets—but nothing prepared her for what awaited her in Room 2912. The door had the do not disturb sign in place, but her clipboard indicated the guest had already checked out. She reached for her master key card, swiping it over the lock, but the door hinges protested as she pushed the door open. The suite was a chaos of overturned furniture, shattered glass, and torn curtains. The air smelled of desperation and fear. The housekeeper clutched her chest, her heart racing. This was no ordinary mess.

And then she saw it—a man's body sprawled across the floor beaten and bleeding from stab wounds. She covered her mouth stifling her scream. The man wore a disheveled suit, blood staining the fabric. His eyes stared into nothingness, pupils wide with shock. The housekeeper recognized him as a guest who'd checked in two days ago. He'd been polite, tipping generously and requesting extra towels.

But now, he lay broken, his life extinguished like a snuffed candle. The room held its breath, as if mourning his passing. The housekeeper's gaze shifted to the shattered mirror above the dresser—a jagged reflection of the violence that had unfolded here.

She reached for the phone, her trembling fingers dialing the front desk.

"This is Daniella," she said, her voice steady despite the chaos around her. "There's been a terrible incident in Room 2912, send help."

As she waited for security, she noticed the ransacked safe—the door hanging open, and a blood-stained envelope on the floor. Had someone else torn through the room, searching for something hidden? The police arrived, their footsteps echoing in the hallway. The housekeeper stepped aside, her gaze lingering on the lifeless form. She'd seen death before, but never like this—violence etched into every corner of the room.

Sergeant McLaughlin escorted her out of the hotel room to get her statement.

Sergeant McLaughlin leaned back in his chair, studying the woman across the table. The interrogation room was sterile, the fluorescent light casting harsh shadows on the gray walls. The suspect, Cassandra Collins, sat with her hands clasped tightly in her lap, her eyes darting between the two Sergeants.

"Cassandra," Sergeant McLaughlin began, his voice calm but probing, "we found your fingerprints at the murder scene. Can you explain that?"

Cassandra's gaze flickered to the one-way mirror, as if seeking an escape. Her knuckles turned white as she gripped the edge of the metal table.

"I don't know how my prints got there. I can't explain it," she said.

Sergeant Jameson, standing by the door, chimed in.

"Cassandra, we also have surveillance footage showing you at the hotel around the time of the murder. Care to explain that?" He asked.

Cassandra's breath hitched. "I was there, yes. But not for anything sinister. I had a meeting."

"What kind of meeting?" McLaughlin leaned forward, his eyes narrowing.

"You wouldn't believe me," Cassandra's voice wavered.

"Cassandra," McLaughlin said softly, "Try us, it would be best to come clean now?"

Cassandra's eyes filled with tears. "He was blackmailing me. I was only there to bring the money. I didn't kill him."

McLaughlin stood, pushing the evidence folder towards her. You're our prime suspect."

As the door closed behind them, Cassandra slumped in her chair, tears streaming down her face. The room felt smaller, suffocating, and unbearable. She wondered if anyone would ever believe her. A police officer came inside the room and placed handcuffs on Cassandra, leading her away.

Four months earlier, Cassandra Collins was excited about the banking convention. She was in a new city, San Diego, and the hotel accommodations were wonderful. Her company, Bank Brussels Lambert, paid all expenses. She checked in at the registration desk, picked up her packet and name badge. This was the chance of a lifetime.

Under the warm glow of the chandeliers in the grand ballroom of the San Diego Convention Center, financial experts, and bank managers from across the world gathered for the annual International Banking Convention. The air hummed with the buzz of multiple languages, the clank of glasses, and the soft shuffling of business cards being exchanged.

Cassandra was a woman of dignity and class, her sharp business insight hidden behind the warm smile she offered to her peers. Her presence at the convention was not just a testament to her personal accomplishments but also a bridge between the bank's celebrated past and the future it had paved the way for.

As she navigated through the crowd, she engaged in discussions about the future of banking, digital currencies, and international finance. The convention was a melting pot of ideas and cultures, much like the city of San Diego itself. Cassandra found herself in a panel discussion, her voice clear and confident as she spoke about the evolving environment of global finance. She drew upon her experiences at Bank Brussels Lambert, her insights shaped by a bank that had navigated the complexities of international monetary exchange and the challenges of a unified European market.

As the day turned to evening, the Pacific Ocean painted the sky with hues of orange and pink, visible through the expansive windows of the convention center. Cassandra stood by the terrace, a glass of champagne in hand, looking out at the horizon. She was more than just a representative of a bank; she was a thinker, ready to lead the charge into a new era of banking, one that promised innovation and growth for all. Cassandra exuded confidence when she spoke, and many people gathered around and followed her during the convention. She was easy to talk to and very approachable, which made her an easy target.

In the bustling atmosphere of the convention, the man leaned against a nearby pillar, his gaze fixed on Cassandra across the room. Sebastian Daniels was the name on his badge provided by the convention. He watched her the very first day as she mingled with other attendees, her confidence radiating as she navigated through the crowd with ease. He observed the way she interacted with others, her laughter punctuating the hum of conversations, her gestures vibrant and assured.

As he prepared to approach, he ran through possible conversation starters in his mind, discarding one after another. He wanted to make an impression, to engage her in a dialogue that would be irresistible. Finally, settling on a topic that would resonate with the theme of the convention, he pushed away from the pillar and made his way towards Cassandra, his steps calculated, his intent sinister.

He reached her just as she was turning, her smile inviting, her attention now on him.

"I couldn't help but notice your insights during the panel discussion," he began, his voice steady. "Your perspective on the subject was fascinating. May I ask how you developed such a distinctive viewpoint?"

And with that, the conversation took off, the initial sizing up, giving way to a fake connection on his part, the convention around them fading into the background as Cassandra was pulled deeper into his web.

"Thank you for such a lively discussion, Sebastian, maybe I will see you tomorrow," Cassandra told him as she headed to her hotel room.

Cassandra called her husband Charles once she made it back to her room. She spent a few minutes on the phone with her son Brian as well.

"Mommy will be home soon sweetheart," she promised.

"How was the first day for you?" Charles asked.

"I met several people in the industry. I'm glad I decided to come but I miss my men," she smiled.

"Goodnight, dear," Charles swooned.

Charles had worked hard to build a career that not only fulfilled him but also provided for his family. He was a software developer at a flourishing tech company, a job that came with a generous salary and flexibility that was rare in this industry. He had crafted a life that many would envy-a well-paying job that bent to his will, allowing him the luxury of time, that most precious commodity to spend with his family whom he loved.

He thought of Cassandra, his partner in every sense of the word, whose laughter was the melody to which his heartbeat. She was the anchor that held him steady in life's tumultuous seas, and the compass that guided him home. In her eyes, he found a love so profound that it often left him breathless. Then there was his son Brian, the brightest star in his sky. Brian was the quiet observer, his thoughtful nature and gentle soul a balm to Charles' own. In Brian's quiet moments of introspection, Charles saw the depth of his son's understanding, far beyond his years.

The next days of the convention consisted of people from all over the world meeting. They were talking and shaking hands, all ready to learn and share ideas about money and banks. A famous money expert talked about how banking around the world is changing and what that means for everyone. People listened carefully as he talked about rules for money that crosses borders, how digital money is changing regular banks, and why it's important to think about the planet when investing money.

There were breakout sessions that Cassandra registered for, one in particular was about how banks help with international trade, talking about things like trade finance and how to avoid risks. Another was about innovative technology in banks, like blockchain, keeping money safe online, and smart programs that help users understand lots of data. Sebastian Daniels was in the same sessions as Cassandra.

"The discussions today have been eye-opening. It's clear that the banking sector must prioritize sustainability and social responsibility to drive growth," he said.

"Absolutely, but we also need to address the reputational risks and ensure that finance serves the greater good," Cassandra replied, impressed with his words.

Cassandra and a few people from the breakout session discussed business over lunch. After lunch some banks and tech companies showed off their newest tools. There were apps for banking on your phone and virtual reality that showed what banking might look like in the future. People explained how these tools make banking easier, better for customers, and follow international rules.

When the day was almost over, everyone started talking and making friends. This was a chance to make deals and start new projects. The convention ended up at the hotel bar area. The group sat at a large booth, laughing, and enjoying light conversation over martinis.

Cassandra nursed the same glass, completely engrossed in each person's story. She laughed at a story one lady relayed about training inexperienced staff.

"Next round of drinks are on me," Sebastian Daniels said.

"I'll have a tequila shot," one man said.

Sebastian Daniels went to the bar ordering drinks for everyone but as he returned to the table, he inconspicuously slipped a white pill in Cassandra's martini glass. He sat down as everyone reached for their respective glass, but he handed Cassandra her martini glass and smiled. After a few sips from the fresh glass, Cassandra began to lose focus, her head swimming.

"Cassandra, are you alright?" Sebastian asked, with false concern.

"My head," she managed, as the group looked on.

"She suffers from allergies, I'll help her to her room," Sebastian lied.

Sebastian assisted Cassandra to get to her hotel room and set his twisted plan into motion. He somehow had access to her room, entering with a key card from his pocket. He strategically had a hidden bag in her room that contained the supplies he needed. He removed her clothes first, deliberately placing them throughout the hotel room, the floor, bed and on the nightstand. He then removed his own clothes, positioning them as well.

He opened the adjourning room door as an unknown figure stepped inside. A camera's flash illuminated the room as it captured image after image. Once the plan was completed, he carefully dressed and rearranged the scene and wiped all surfaces to remove fingerprints. He exited the hotel room as if he were never there.

Cassandra replayed the blurred memories of that day like a broken record repeating itself over and over again. She remembered the hurt she felt when she opened the envelope that changed her life forever. She was a fool for trusting a stranger, yet Cassandra had failed to trust her friend Naomi with the truth when it first happened and now, she was being accused of murder. She didn't know who else to trust.

Cassandra then remembered the name of the private investigation agency Naomi worked for, but she dreaded making the phone call. Cassandra did not know how to face speaking with Naomi. Cassandra was relieved when she got voicemail, so she left a message instead of having to actually speak to someone in person.

It had been nearly six months since Naomi's first case as a private investigator. So much had occurred in such a brief period in her life once she moved back to New Orleans. Henry Williams' betrayal had been a harsh lesson, but it had also been the catalyst for Naomi to rediscover herself. His betrayal had made her question her judgment, her ability to read people, skills crucial to being an investigator. The betrayal became a chapter in her story, a painful memory that no longer held power over her. But Naomi grew wiser, more discerning, and understood that sometimes, those closest to you can have the most damaging agendas. She pledged to never let her guard down again and to build her future career on the foundation of integrity and transparency.

Her former boss, Theodore Miller never returned from Honduras. Instead, he retired from the agency due to personal business, transferring the business over to Naomi. The first big case she closed earned her a stellar reputation with both the FBI and local law enforcement. Referral cases came to the agency daily.

Maragret Regis was an asset that Naomi had come to appreciate. Margaret Regis grew up in the vibrant heart of New Orleans, where the city's pulse was as familiar to her as her own heartbeat. The middle child in a family of seven, she learned early on the art of observation—how to listen more than speak, and how to notice the details others might miss. These skills served her well in her youth, helping her navigate the complex social waters of her neighborhood. As she entered her mid-forties Margaret found herself at a crossroads. Her children were grown up, and the house was quiet, too quiet. Her husband, a once-promising jazz musician, had settled into the comfortable routine of teaching music at the local high school.

Margaret longed for something more, a spark to reignite the sense of purpose she once felt. That's when she met Theodore Miller, a seasoned private investigator with a reputation for solving the cases that left the New Orleans Police Department scratching their heads.

Theodore recognized Margaret's keen eye for detail and her intuitive understanding of human nature. He offered her a job as his assistant, and she accepted without hesitation. Working at New Orleans Private Investigation, INC, Margaret found her call. She wasn't just Theodore's assistant; she was his confidante, his strategist, and often, his secret weapon. With her deep knowledge of the city and its people, Margaret could navigate the underbelly of New Orleans as easily as she could its sunlit streets. She had a knack for finding the threads that connected seemingly unrelated cases, and her gentle manner often coaxed out truths that others couldn't reach.

Margaret's life was not without its challenges. The world of private investigation was unpredictable, and danger lurked in the shadows of the cases she helped solve. But for Margaret, each mystery solved brought satisfaction that she couldn't find anywhere else. In the intricate dance of light and dark that was New Orleans, Margaret Regis had found her stage. Theodore Miller confided in Margaret that he needed to settle his friend's estate back home in Honduras so he brought in Naomi Bloom who would soon replace him. Despite their shaky start, Margaret would come to respect Naomi as much if not greater than Theodore.

Naomi and the agency handled more than 30 cases in four months, so many that Sheila Harris was busy training fresh staff as Naomi sat contemplating changing the name of the agency since she now had multiple investigators working for her and she had taken on a partner. The agency also had a new location in Downtown New Orleans in the heart of the city to accommodate its expansion.

Sheila Harris was born and raised on the vibrant streets of New Orleans, Sheila Harris grew up amidst the echoes of jazz and the mysteries of the bayou. Her childhood was a tapestry of Mardi Gras parades and the haunting tales of the French Quarter, which fueled her imagination and a deep-seated curiosity. Sheila's mother, a renowned Creole chef, instilled in her a love for the city's rich culture and history, while her father, a local historian, shared with her the darker stories and legends that the cobblestone streets whispered at night. It was this blend of beauty and mystery that led Sheila to her passion for uncovering truths hidden beneath layers of secrets.

After studying criminal psychology at Tulane University, Sheila found herself drawn to the world of private investigation. She began her career as secretary to Theodore Miller at the New Orleans Private Investigation, INC , a small but reputable firm known for solving some of the most puzzling cases in the city.

Sheila's role at the agency grew to more than just administrative. Now under Naomi Bloom's guidance her keen eye for detail, ability to read people, and her knowledge of the city's streets made her an invaluable resource.

Sheila was often found poring over case files, connecting dots that others missed, and using her charm to gather information from the most tight-lipped of sources. As a single woman in a city that danced to its own beat, Sheila cherished her independence to a degree. She lived in a quaint shotgun house in the Marigny neighborhood, with her loyal dog, Roux, a dark chocolate lab and an impressive collection of detective novels that would rival the agency's own archives.

By day, Sheila was a poised and efficient assistant, managing the chaos of the agency with a steady hand, but by night she was a student of the city, exploring its hidden corners and learning its secrets, and she had a side investigation going, trying to find out all she could about Joseph Kensington, her secret office crush.

Taylor wore two hats for the agency, attorney, and investigator in training, working toward his official investigator certification which required 3 years of experience. Taylor's law office handled any minor cases that required legal assistance, while Naomi and the other investigators handled the others. After the narrow escape with the Debugger investigation, Taylor decided to play a pivotal role in the agency, accompanying Naomi on potentially dangerous cases or enlisting one of his two friends, Joseph Kensington, or Anthony Wheaton. The two welcomed the freelance work, and the retainer fee was top-notch.

Joseph was a man of few words, but his silence was not mistaken for a lack of depth and beneath his stoic exterior was a tumultuous sea of intrigue.

Joseph's life was a mosaic of secrets, pieced together from years of observing others from the dark corners of the city. A former intelligence officer, Joseph, had traded in a badge for a more subtle form of investigation. As a private consultant he made his own rules. One evening, while tracking a wayward husband through the vibrant chaos of Bourbon Street, Joseph's path crossed with that of Taylor Sylvester, a prominent attorney known for his sharp mind and sharper suits. Taylor, with his keen legal acumen, had sensed he was being followed for days, a feeling unshakeable even amidst the courtroom's order.

Their meeting was a collision of worlds—Joseph, the watcher, and Taylor, the defender. Over chicory coffee and beignets, they found an unlikely friendship. Taylor was intrigued by Joseph's world, so different from the structured life of law he knew. Joseph, in turn, saw in Taylor a man of integrity, a rare find in the shadows they both navigated. As their friendship deepened, so did their collaboration. Taylor's cases often led him to the doorsteps of those who preferred to remain hidden, and Joseph's skills in surveillance became an invaluable asset.

Together, they became an unspoken alliance, a force that tread the fine line between the letter of the law and the spirit of justice. In the heart of the city, where secrets were currency, Joseph and Taylor learned to trust the unspoken bond that tied them. For in New Orleans, it wasn't just about what you knew, but also about who you watched over in the silent hours of the night.

Anthony was fiercely loyal to Taylor. Anthony Wheaton, a former Navy SEAL, found solace in the city's chaotic embrace. His broad shoulders and the disciplined set of his jaw were telltale signs of his military past, but his eyes, a piercing black, held stories untold. Anthony had come to New Orleans seeking anonymity, a place where his past could be just another tale in the city's tapestry of history. But trouble, as it often does, found him on a balmy evening at a local jazz bar. A misunderstanding escalated, and before he knew it, Anthony was facing charges that could unravel the quiet life he had carefully built but Taylor Sylvester stepped in. Taylor was an attorney with a sharp mind and a sharper tongue who could read a room like a book and had the uncanny ability to find the truth hidden within a web of lies. He was a local, born and bred in the heart of the city, with a love for its culture and a passion for justice.

Their paths crossed in the most unexpected of ways. Taylor had been at the bar that night, a silent observer of the chaos that unfolded. He saw something in Anthony, a sense of honor that contested the situation. When the opportunity arose to represent Anthony, Taylor took it without hesitation. As they worked together to navigate the muddy waters of the legal system, a friendship formed between the two men. They were an unlikely pair: Anthony, with his stoic silence and military precision, and Taylor, with his easy charm and quick wit. Yet, they found common ground in their mutual respect and the unspoken understanding of what it meant to serve—Anthony his country, Taylor the law.

Their conversations often lingered after the meetings, drifting from strategies and evidence to life and philosophy. Anthony learned of Taylor's dreams to reform the legal system, to make it more just for those who had no voice. Taylor, in turn, discovered Anthony's love for the ocean, the way he missed the camaraderie of his SEAL team, and his struggle to find purpose in civilian life. The bond between Anthony and Taylor grew stronger. They were no longer just a former SEAL and an attorney; they were brothers-in-arms, fighting a different kind of battle. And in the heart of New Orleans, a city that had seen its share of battles, they stood side by side, ready to face whatever came their way. In Anthony's line of work, he never married or had a committed relationship. Anthony ran a small security consulting firm, offering his expertise in weapons training and martial arts. Both he and Joseph were like Taylor's brothers and now they would soon be gaining a sister-in-law in Naomi.

Chapter 2

"Taylor!" She yelled from their adjoining office. "What name should we give the agency?"

Taylor Sylvester, Naomi's fiancé, and now, her new business partner contemplated her question.

"We have plenty of time to decide on a new name for the agency after the wedding," he called back.

Friday had arrived and their wedding was a week away. Naomi was keeping her mind busy with paperwork as she wrapped up the day. She meticulously organized all of her closed cases, preparing them for Margaret Regis to file away. She shredded any extraneous papers from her desk before she would head out for the weekend. Today was both of their last day of work. Naomi and Taylor had planned to take a break from the agency before and after the wedding.

Taylor sat at his large mahogany desk finalizing some last-minute preparations for their big day. He was in charge of travel arrangements and hotel accommodations for their out-of-town guests. He contacted the hotel to make sure the ballroom décor would be to his exact specifications for the wedding reception. He also reserved an entire side of the hotel for family and friends. Taylor was meticulously detailed in all facets of his life with extremely ambitious standards. The food and cake tasting was completed weeks ago by the couple but yet he contacted both the caterer and bakery to ensure everything was in place.

Taylor and Naomi left the agency together to sit and unwind after a long week in preparation for their special upcoming nuptials. Taylor made 7:30 dinner reservations which allowed time for them to stop home, shower and change clothes. Taylor admired everything about Naomi as he watched her prepare for her shower. His future wife smiled when she caught a glimpse of him looking in her direction. Since he always had to be the last to get dressed, she obliged him and headed to shower only to be accompanied by him moments later.

"We can't break our promise," she nervously said.

"We won't," he whispered, stepping alongside her.

The steam enveloped the bathroom in a warm mist, concealing the lines between reality and the dream-like state they found themselves in. The gentle drumming of water from the showerhead played a soothing rhythm, the sound a soft backdrop to their secluded world. Naomi's laughter echoed off the tiles, a melody more delightful to Taylor than the symphony of droplets around them. He watched her, the way the water cascaded over her shoulders, tracing the contours of her body before pooling at their feet. The dim light cast a golden glow, giving her skin a delicate radiance.

"Come here," he mouthed, his voice barely rising above the hum of the shower.

Naomi stepped closer, the space between them disappearing with her movement. He reached out, his fingers brushing against her cheek, tracing the path of a single droplet that dared to stray from the others. She closed her eyes, leaning into his touch, a relaxing sigh escaping her lips. The world outside disappeared away, leaving only the two of them, the warmth of the water, and the promise of a love as enduring as an endless ring. In that moment, under the cascade of water and passion, they found a sanctuary, a haven within each other's arms.

Taylor didn't break their promise, but they stood there for what felt like an eternity, communicating in the language of touch and presence. It was a moment of pure connection, unmarked by the difficulties of life. In the simplicity of the shower, they discovered a sanctuary where words were unnecessary. As the water turned from warm to cool, they reluctantly stepped out, wrapping themselves in towels. But the heat they carried within them, the warmth of their love, remained unaffected by the chill of the air. After their shower, they quickly dressed and left the house for dinner.

At dinner Naomi and Taylor sat close to one another smiling, enjoying each other's company. The meal was a quiet affair, each course presented with care but without fanfare. The conversation flowed like the wine, gentle and unhurried. They spoke of dreams and memories; their voices were barely above a whisper as if too loud a word would shatter the serenity of the evening.

"You haven't looked at your phone one time during dinner," Taylor remarked.

"I am all yours Mr. Sylvester," Naomi smiled proudly.

"That is good to know," Taylor smiled back.

Taylor and Naomi headed home for the night to conclude their Friday. Naomi was the happiest she had been in months. They talked for hours about their future dreams and the family they would have.

As the moonlight streamed through the sheer curtains, casting a soft glow over the room, Naomi and Taylor lay intertwined in the comfort of their bed, a cocoon of warmth in the cool night. The air was thick with anticipation, the kind that precedes a life-altering event. They would soon be married, their separate lives weaving into one tapestry.

Naomi's head rested on Taylor's chest, listening to the steady rhythm of his heart, a reassurance of the constant in her life.

"What do you think our future will look like?" She whispered, her voice barely audible over the sound of the crickets serenading the night.

Taylor took a moment, his fingers tracing idle patterns on her back.

"I see us in a welcoming home, filled with children and laughter and the smell of your Sunday morning French toast," he began, the corners of his mouth turning into a smile.

"And a dog?" Naomi lifted her head, her eyes sparkling with hope.

"At least one," Taylor chuckled. "A big friendly one that'll greet us at the door and hog the bed."

Naomi nestled closer, her smile deepening. "I'd prefer one I can cuddle with, you already hog the bed and definitely children," she agreed.

"In time," he said, his voice tender. "Little adventurers with your beautiful spirit and, hopefully, my sense of direction."

"I can envision family vacations to sunny places, with amusement parks and nature walks," Naomi laughed.

"Your laughter is music to my ears. I can't wait to grow old with you," Taylor said, gently kissing her lips.

They fell into a comfortable silence, each lost in one another's dreams of a shared future. The night was a blank canvas, and their words painted pictures of hope, love, and the infinite possibilities that awaited them. As sleep began to claim them, Naomi moved closer into Taylor's embrace, their last thoughts were of gratitude for the love they had found in each other and the life they would soon build together, an indication of the belief that the future, no matter how uncertain, was theirs to shape however they imagined it could be.

Naomi visited her mother Saturday morning for the final fitting of her wedding dress, which was her weekly routine. Naomi assisted her mother with beading the handmade wedding gown. She enjoyed their Saturday morning conversation as both women stitched tiny pearls on the antique lace.

"Naomi, you are going to be the most gorgeous, elegant bride, I hope that groom of yours is ready," her mother laughed.

She shared a quaint brunch with her mother, consisting of shrimp and grits, French toast, and hot café au lait. Once brunch was completed, she and her mother carefully stored her delicate wedding dress in an oversized bridal garment bag. Naomi kissed her mother, grateful for their inseparable bond and the special time shared making her wedding gown. She headed back to New Orleans to prepare for the evening festivities. The bachelor and bachelorette parties were organized for Saturday night by the best man and matron of honor. The two had specific instructions from bride and groom for both events.

As the wedding countdown dwindled, Saturday evening Naomi's bridal party, led by Michelle, her matron of honor, gathered for the bachelorette party. The evening sun dipped below the horizon, casting a soft golden glow over the city as the ladies arrived at the rooftop garden of the luxurious Omni Royal Orleans. The air was scented with jasmine and the gentle strumming of a harp blended with the laughter of old and new friends reuniting, awaiting the bride.

Naomi stepped out of the shiny, black limousine, her white chiffon dress waving in the gentle breeze. She entered the hotel lobby and checked in with the hotel staff to make them aware of her arrival. Her closest friends, adorned in elegant cocktail dresses, gathered around, as Naomi stepped from the elevator. The rooftop was a vision of elegance, with white roses and magnolias in full bloom giving off their sweet aroma, crystal chandeliers hanging from trellises, and tables draped in ivory silk cloths. A private chef from Sheila's mother's restaurant prepared delicate hors d'oeuvres while a bartender presented a selection of delicious cocktails adorned with fresh cut fruit.

As the night unfolded, the women shared stories and reminisced about their college days, their voices mingling with the soft jazz playing in the background. They toasted to Naomi's future, with each clink of their glasses an indication of the unique bond they each shared with her. For a special gift to Naomi, Michelle arranged for a local artist to capture the celebration on canvas, their brushstrokes preserving the special moment forever. The party was not about wild antics or embarrassing dares; it was a celebration of love, friendship, and the journey ahead, exactly to Naomi's specifications. The women made their way to the balcony, where they danced under the moonlight, their silhouettes reflecting off the shimmering roof top pool, enjoying the music as their laughter echoed into the night.

As the golden tones of the setting sun brushed the marble façade of its outside, Taylor's bachelor party was unfolding not with raucous revelry, but with the refined elegance befitting the man of the hour. The venue was The New Orleans Museum of Arts, closed to the public for this private celebration. Inside, the museum had transformed from a sanctuary of art to a sanctuary of sophistication and revelry. The main gallery, now dimly lit, was adorned with tasteful decorations that complemented the masterpieces on the walls, and the air hummed with a jazz band's rendition of Taylor's favorite songs.

The guests, a select group of Taylor's closest friends, were a mix of influential attorneys, tech moguls, and fraternity brothers. They mingled among the sculptures and paintings, whiskey glasses in hand, discussing a vast variety of topics. Taylor was an avid whiskey connoisseur so nestled in one corner, a whiskey bar offered tastings of rare single malts, each accompanied by a sommelier's expert notes. Nearby, a gourmet chef prepared a series of small plates, each a tiny work of culinary art, combining both Creole and Cajun flavors that left the men in silent appreciation. Taylor, ever the gracious host despite being the evening's honoree, ensured everyone felt welcome, their glasses never empty, their palates always full. As the evening progressed, the conversation shifted from the intellectual to the personal, stories of Taylor's college days bringing laughter and the sincerity of shared memories.

As the night waned, the party found its way to the museum's courtyard. Under a canopy of stars and amidst the sculptures, the jazz band took up their instruments. The band swelled, a lively second-line tune that invited the men to shed their inhibitions, waving white handkerchiefs. The night was a tapestry of moments, each more memorable than the last. It was a bachelor party that paid homage to the city's culture, to friendship, and to the art of living well. As the moon climbed higher in the sky, the gentlemen departed, knowing they had celebrated Taylor in a manner appropriate for the man he was and the husband he would soon become.

The days leading up to the wedding were a string of emotions all around, woven with threads of excitement, anticipation, and a touch of anxiety. Naomi found herself caught in a flurry of last-minute preparations; each day marked by a list that seemed to grow rather than shrink. Taylor, on the other hand, was entrenched in his own rituals, from final fittings of his custom tuxedo to heartfelt conversations with his best man, Lucious. Each moment a step closer to the life he was about to embrace.

Amid it all, the couple found stolen moments of tranquility, where the world fell away, and it was just the two of them. They spoke of the future, of hopes and dreams, of the journey they were about to embark upon together. A permanent smile was fixed on Naomi's face as she awaited her wedding day.

Their rehearsal dinner was scheduled for the Friday before the wedding, for early afternoon at a local restaurant Taylor reserved. Taylor was friends with the owner and chef of the restaurant. He arranged for the finest accommodations for the evening. The guest list included the bridal party, family, and close friends. Dinner guests entered the newly renovated restaurant to find elegantly set tables arranged in a circular formation with the head table positioned in the center. The soft murmur of conversations filled the air as guests mingled, their laughter punctuating the gentle hum of the jazz quartet in the corner.

At the head table Taylor sat looking stoic in his tailored suit, his hand occasionally reaching out to squeeze Naomi's lovingly. Naomi was radiant in a flowing dress of cream and lace, her eyes sparkling with eagerness. The aroma of Creole flavors wafted from the open kitchen, promising a feast of New Orleans delicacies. Waiters in crisp black uniforms slid between the tables, pouring glasses of champagne, and offering appetizers on silver platters. As the evening progressed the best man stood, tapping his glass gently. The room fell silent, all eyes turning to him.

"Ladies and Gentlemen if I could have your attention for just a moment. As we gather here on the eve of what is sure to be a beautiful and memorable day, I'd like to raise my glass to two of the most wonderful people I've had the privilege of knowing. To Taylor, my best friend, my brother, confidant, and the man who is brave enough to wear his heart on his sleeve. You've always been the one to lead the way, whether it was for fun or towards success, and now, you're leading us into a celebration of love.

And to Naomi, thank you for not only stealing his heart but for being the reason his smile is just that much brighter. You've embraced his eccentricities, laughed at his jokes, and most importantly, you've loved him unconditionally. Together, you are a testament to the fact that true love not only exists but thrives when nurtured by kindness, laughter, and an endless supply of inside jokes.

So, let's toast to the moments that brought them together, the love that has blossomed, and the journey that lies ahead. May your love be modern enough to survive the times and old-fashioned enough to last forever.

Cheers to Taylor and Naomi!" Lucious concluded.

The rehearsal dinner continued into the night, a celebration of love, family, and the promise of a beautiful tomorrow. Taylor stood, tapping his whisky glass to get the guests' attention. The room fell to a hush as he began toast to his bride-to-be.

"To my bride-to-be, the love of my life, you have captivated my heart by being exactly who you are: the sweetest, most loving, and compassionate person I have ever known. You inspire me every day with your kindness, your laughter, and your unwavering support. I am beyond excited to begin this new chapter with you, and I promise to cherish and honor you for all the days of my life. Family and friends, I never knew that loving this beautiful woman could be so easy. With Naomi at my side, I have found my undeniable soulmate." Taylor sealed his toast with a long drink from his glass.

Naomi rose from her seat alongside Taylor filled with emotions, lifting her glass, "I am blessed for every step that led me to this amazing man I plan to call my husband. Taylor, you have been my rock since the day I ran into you on the street so many years ago. You are always in my corner cheering me on. Tomorrow cannot come soon enough." She ended her toast, sipping from her wine glass.

The guests erupted into applause which turned into jovial laughter as the celebration continued onto a makeshift dance floor. The music came alive as the couple danced among family and friends. It could not have been a more special occasion. At the end of the evening Naomi and Taylor parted ways until their wedding.

Chapter 3

Naomi and Michelle headed to the hotel and entered their luxury suite. Naomi's night was restful, filled with excitement and dreams of what was to come, and when dawn broke, it was not just a new day that beckoned, but a new chapter waiting to be written. Naomi enjoyed the time she and Michelle shared; she was able to have a quiet morning just to be still. That morning the two enjoyed a catered breakfast with all of Naomi's favorites, Taylor coordinated every detail. After breakfast and a long spa treatment, Naomi stood before the mirror of her hotel suite, the reflection gazing back at her not just a bride, but a montage of all the roles she had ever played - daughter, sister, friend, and now, soon to be wife.

Naomi, can you believe the day is finally here? You look absolutely stunning," Michelle said.

"Thank you! I can't believe it either. It feels like we were just in college, dreaming about this day and now it's here," Naomi blushed.

"I know, right? All those plans and dreams, and you've made them come true. Taylor's a lucky man," Michelle smiled.

"I'm the lucky one. But I couldn't have done any of this without you," Naomi said.

"That's what best friends are for, to hold your hand when you're nervous," Michelle said.

"I am a bit nervous," Naomi confessed.

"It's normal to be nervous. But once you walk down that aisle and see Taylor waiting for you, all the nerves will melt away," Michelle assured her.

"I hope so. I just want everything to be perfect," Naomi told her.

"It will be, because it's a celebration of you and the love you two share. Perfection is in imperfections, remember." Michelle smiled.

"You always know what to say Michelle. Thank you for being here, for everything," Naomi said.

"Always. Now, let's get you dressed and married!" Michelle told her.

The air was thick with the sweet scent of magnolias and the sun cast a golden hue over the historic French Quarter. Wedding guests arrayed in light linen suits and summer dresses gathered under a canopy of strung lights in a secluded courtyard, surrounded by the weathered brick walls of an elegant Creole mansion. Taylor eagerly awaited Naomi's entrance as jazz band set the mood with their rendition of "Our Love Is Here to Stay," their notes floating through the balmy afternoon air. His eyes brimmed with anticipation, trying his best to contain his emotions.

The aisle was lined with white rose petals, mixed with jasmine and gardenias as well, all of her favorites. Naomi, radiant in a vintage lace gown, hand sewn by her mother and beaded by the two of them, made her way gracefully, her veil trailing behind like a soft cloud. She was the epitome of beauty. The wedding gown was exquisite, delicately hugging every curve of Naomi's body. The bodice sculpted to her form as if it were a second skin adorned with delicate beading that caught the light with every movement. The neckline, demure, yet alluring, framed her collarbones subtly exposing a hint of cleavage.

Taylor felt a catch in his breath, a tightening in his broad chest that wasn't from his custom tuxedo. He nervously cleared his throat as the music began to play. It was as if time slowed, each second extending into eternity as Naomi took her first step down the aisle. Taylor watched in awe as she slowly made her way to his outstretched hand. As a wedding surprise he began to sing the song he wrote for Naomi.

"Like a song of love that clings to me
how the thought of you does things to me,
never felt this way Naomi, I'm so alive
as you walk toward me my beautiful bride.
Naomi, you're the rhythm to my melody,
The sweetest note in life's symphony,
As you glide down the aisle, so gracefully,
My heart sways to your love's harmony.
Naomi you are my sun, my moon, my endless sky
Your love lifts me higher it makes me fly,
With every step you take my soul ignites
My bride my love you are my sweet delight."

SHATTERED DREAMS

This was not a part of what they rehearsed and caught Naomi completely off guard because they never planned for a soloist at their wedding, then she realized the smooth baritone sounds were coming from Taylor. With each sultry note Taylor sang, the congregation leaned forward, captivated by the groom's soulful voice. Some closed their eyes, lost in the melody, while others exchanged knowing glances. The older guests reminisced about their own passionate beginnings, and the younger ones dream of love stories yet to unfold. Naomi tried to contain her emotions as she moved to the melody of his voice. Taylor could see the gentle shimmer of tears in her eyes as she approached him. He continued to sing,

"Your lips, a forbidden fruit I crave,
Tasting of moonlight and secrets saved,
Our bodies, like notes in a sultry wave,
A symphony of desire and passion engraved.
I've waited a lifetime for this day,
To see you in white, my soul's ballet,
Your smile, a spotlight that won't fade away,
Forever written in my heart, come what may.
Naomi you are my sun, my moon, my endless sky
Your love lifts me higher it makes me fly,
With every step you take my soul ignites
My bride my love you are my sweet delight.
And so, we stand two souls intertwined,
in this love story forever written in time
as you become my wife my heart you own
I'll sing this love song for you alone.
As you float down the aisle my heart takes flight
a vision of grace, bathed in soft sunlight,
Your eyes meet mine and time stands still
in this sacred moment I know it's real
Naomi you are my sun, my moon, my endless sky
Your love lifts me higher it makes me fly,
With every step you take my soul ignites
My bride my love you are my sweet delight."

Naomi's heart fluttered like a caged bird each time Taylor mentioned her name. Her eyes remained fixed on him, as he sang with a passion that ignited every emotion inside of her. In that moment, she relived their shared memories—the stolen kisses, whispered promises, and moonlit rendezvouses. The wedding guests faded into a distant hum; all that mattered was their love. Her fingers trembled against the bouquet, and she no longer wondered how deeply he loved her. As the final chords lingered, Naomi stepped forward, ready to stay forever in the warmth of his velvet whispers.

As Naomi reached the customed wedding arch, she mouthed "I love you" to him. Taylor stood proudly, staring at the vision of loveliness that was before him. As they exchanged vows, the sky transitioned from golden to a canvas of pastel pinks and purples, the first stars beginning to twinkle faintly above. The evening was magical, a true fairytale come true. Taylor took his time when he was able to finally kiss his bride, tenderly kissing her soft mouth anticipating what was to come later. They promised to abstain from sexual activity until their wedding day to make their wedding night union exceptional. Taylor lifted Naomi and carried her to an awaiting horse-drawn carriage, their official escort to the wedding reception a few blocks away.

"Taylor I never knew you could sing like that," Naomi beamed, genuinely impressed and amazed. She had only heard him hum or sing along to songs here and there.

"There is a lot to learn about me," he told her, as he leaned in to kiss his bride, a kiss that seemed to last the entire ride.

As the horse-drawn carriage rolled to a gentle stop, Taylor extended his hand to help his blushing bride step down. Naomi's gown rustled softly as she moved towards him, and her eyes sparkled with eagerness to partake in the festivities awaiting them. The guests gathered, their whispers hushed, as the couple walked together holding hands—a symbol of love and new beginnings.

Inside at the reception, the clink of glasses and soft laughter filled the air as the newlyweds shared their first dance, their silhouettes a picture of love against the flickering candlelight. Taylor whispered the words to their favorite song in her ear, as they swayed to the music. He held her body close to his as they moved in unison. Naomi and Taylor were a stunning couple, admired by friends and family alike. The couple posed for pictures to commemorate their special day. After numerous rounds of hors d'oeuvres being passed, they moved on to the dinner buffet which consisted of an array of creole and Cajun specialties. Once it was time to cut the cake for their guests to enjoy the sweet dessert, Taylor and Naomi shared the first piece of cake, playfully feeding one another.

Their reception was transformed into a late-evening dance party. Naomi enjoyed good music and loved to dance; the music took control as she controlled the dance floor. Taylor enjoyed watching his bride move to the rhythmic vibes. He joined in for only slow ballads, taking advantage of every opportunity to have her body close to his. The celebration continued into the night, the joyous energy of New Orleans held the couple and their guests in a warm, unforgettable embrace. Naomi and Taylor said farewells to their guests as they exited the reception to cheers and wishes from all.

The elevator doors slid open with a soft chime, and Taylor emerged with his bride, cradling her gently in his arms. Her wedding gown cascaded over his shoulder, and she clung to his neck, laughing softly as they approached the door of their hotel suite.

"Ready for the grand entrance Mrs. Sylvester?" Taylor asked, his eyes flickering with joy.

Naomi nodded, her cheeks flushed with happiness. "I've been waiting so long for this moment," she replied, her voice a melodic whisper.

With a quick, playful movement, Taylor shifted her weight slightly and reached for the door handle. As the door swung open, he stepped across the threshold, carrying Naomi into the suite. The room was bathed in a warm, golden light, and the air was filled with the subtle scent of magnolia.

Taylor carefully set Naomi down on her feet, and she took a moment to take in their fancy surroundings. The suite was elegantly decorated, with lavish furnishings, soft lighting, and a magnificent view of the city skyline through floor-to-ceiling windows.

"It's perfect," Naomi breathed, her eyes shining with delight.

Taylor wrapped his arms around her from behind, resting his chin on her shoulder. "Just like you," he murmured, pressing a soft kiss to her cheek.

They stood there for a moment, savoring the intimacy of the moment and the start of their new life together. The journey that had brought them to this point felt like a beautiful dream, and the promise of their future was just as enchanting.

"How about we toast to us?" Taylor proposed, breaking the comfortable silence. He moved to the small table by the window, where a bottle of Cristal Rose and two glasses waited. He cleverly uncorked the bottle, and the champagne bubbled up as he poured it into the glasses.

They clinked their glasses together, their smiles reflecting the love and excitement in their hearts. "To us," they said in unison, and then took a sip.

Outside, the world was hushed, as if in respect of the intimateness of the moment unfolding within. Taylor took the glass from Naomi's hand and a rush of nerves overcome her. Their promise of abstinence was over, a celebration of their love was near, a moment they had yearned for through hints and vows. As they stepped into the bedroom, the world outside faded away, leaving only the two of them, enveloped in the shelter of their devotion.

The bed was draped in the finest silk sheets, a palette of pearl and purples that whispered of warmth and luxury. Rose petals were scattered across the pillows, a trail leading to the balcony where the night sky was a canvas of stars, each one a silent witness to the couple's union.

Naomi was nervous, her body trembled, she could feel her heart pounding in her chest. She took a deep breath, trying to calm her nerves.

"Why am I so nervous?" she whispered to herself.

"You so look beautiful," Taylor told her, sensing her anxiousness. "Hey," he said softly, his voice filled with concern. "What's on your mind?"

"I don't know," she admitted, her voice trembling. "It's just... everything feels so overwhelming. The wedding, the ceremony, and now we're finally alone, and it feels like a lot to take in," she confided what was in her heart. Expressing her feelings out loud actually eased her nerves.

Naomi felt a wave of relief wash over her at his words. She leaned her back into him, resting her head on his chest.

"We have the rest of our lives to figure things out. And we'll do it one step at a time," Taylor told her.

"Thank you," she murmured. "I'm so lucky to have you."

Taylor helped Naomi undo her wedding dress, slowly one hook at a time. He held her close to his warm body to ease her shakiness. Taylor was her private sanctuary. Her soft body caressed against the firmness of his form, a stark contrast with one another. He gently pulled her closer, wrapping his arms around her.

"We don't have to rush," he whispered. "We have all the time in the world. Let's just enjoy being together."

She leaned into him, resting her head on his chest. The steady rhythm of his heartbeat soothed her, and she felt her nerves begin to melt away.

"I love you," she murmured.

"I love you too," Taylor replied, his voice filled with sincerity.

He tilted her chin up, meeting her gaze. Slowly, he leaned in and kissed her, the soft brush of his full lips sending shivers down her spine. Their kiss deepened, growing more passionate as they lost themselves in each other. Taylor's hands gently caressed her back, while Naomi's fingers twirled in his thick hair. The world outside seemed to disappear, leaving only the two of them in their intimate surroundings. Their kisses grew more passionate, each touch igniting a fire within them. As they explored the newfound intimacy of husband and wife, they both knew that this was just the beginning of a lifetime of love and connection. In that moment, surrounded by the warmth and love they shared, they felt a permanent bond that would carry them through anything life had to offer.

Taylor rediscovered every inch of wife's body with delicate precision. Their bodies moved effortlessly together, a loving dance of souls merging into one, a melody of sighs and soft laughter that filled the room with the harmony of their love. Their wedding night unfolded like a dream, a series of moments etched in the soft glow of candlelight. They explored the depths of their love, each touch a new discovery, each kiss a treasure uncovered. Time ceased to exist, measured only by the beating of their hearts and the breathless wonder of their embrace.

As dawn approached, they lay intertwined, a tangle of limbs and sheets, the embers of their passion still warm between them. The first light of morning crept through the curtains, casting a magical hue over their slumbering forms. And in that tranquil silence, they found peace, knowing that this was just the beginning of their life.

Naomi awoke first at 8:00 AM to the soft chirp of the alarm, a satisfied peaceful smile was on her face as she watched her husband sleep, silently counting each breath he took. She replayed their wedding night in her mind waiting for him to wake from his sleep. She lay admiring her perfectly manicured hand, adorned with the new wedding band nestled against her flawless engagement ring, a perfect pair she thought, just like the two of them.

Taylor quietly moaned as he stirred from his peaceful rest, smiling when he saw Naomi admiring her ring.

"Good morning to you Mrs. Sylvester," he crooned in a smooth voice.

"Good morning Mr. Sylvester, that has such a wonderful ring to it," she said through a toothy smile.

"We have a few hours before we head to the airport, are you ready for breakfast?" Taylor asked his wife.

"French toast and a side of you," she said, playfully pulling the covers over their heads.

After an encore performance of last night, they showered and dressed, preparing for breakfast and the airport trip for their honeymoon. The trip to Fiji would take them 14 hours but it would be well worth the time. Paradise awaited Naomi and Taylor. His preparation and attention to detail surpassed her every want and desire. Taylor spared no expense where Naomi was concerned, but he never flaunted his wealth which he inherited from his grandfather. In lieu of a destination wedding, he chartered a special private jet for their trip because he wanted his wife all to himself.

As their morning flight crept across the horizon, the sleek private jet sliced through the pillow like clouds, its silver wings glinting in the brilliant sunlight. Inside the private cabin, nestled in the plush leather seats, Taylor and Naomi sat hand in hand, embarking on their first adventure as a married couple. Naomi's eyes were wide with wonder as she pressed her face against the cool window, watching the world transform below them. The ocean stretched out, an endless canvas of blues, its waves whispering promises of paradise. Taylor, ever the romantic, had surprised her with this luxurious escape to Fiji, a place where they could lose themselves in each other and the beauty of nature.

The flight attendant, with a smile as warm as the Fijian sun, offered them a glass of champagne, the bubbles dancing like their shared laughter. They toasted to love, to life, and to the endless possibilities yet to come. As they clinked glasses, the jet soared higher, carrying them away from the familiar and towards the unknown.

Taylor leaned over, his lips softly brushing Naomi's ear.

"To us," he whispered, his voice a melody over the soft jazz playing in the background.

Naomi turned to him, her eyes sparkling with excitement.

"To us," she echoed, sipping from the glass.

They sealed their toast with a long kiss. Naomi's heart was soaring as high as the jet. The world below was a blur, but up in the jet, everything was crystal clear. They were together, they were in love, and they were on their way to a slice of heaven. Fiji awaited, with its white sandy beaches, its clear turquoise waters, and its promise of a honeymoon they would never forget.

Naomi and Taylor were able to talk and connect on a new level during the first hours of their flight, drifting off to sleep mid-conversation, waking for lunch and drinks, basking in each other's company. The private jet, a bastion of luxury and intimacy, offered Taylor and Naomi an unmatched experience as they journeyed through the night skies.

The cabin was filled with an air of relaxed luxury. The private jet cruised steadily over the Pacific Ocean, the waves below shimmering like liquid silver under the light of the moon. The setting sun had painted the sky in hues of lavender and gold, a fitting prelude to the romantic evening ahead. A small table, set near the expansive windows, was dressed elegantly with crisp white linen, gleaming silverware, and crystal glasses. A vase with filled with fragrant plumeria flowers symbolizing Fiji's tropical beauty, sat in the center, their pink and white petals echoing the warmth of their feelings for one another.

The flight attendant presented the first course: a platter of fresh sashimi paired with a honey-soy dressing, reminiscent of the flavors waiting for them in Fiji. Each bite was delicate yet bursting with taste, perfectly complemented by the crisp white wine that followed. But it wasn't just about the food, it was the way their hands brushed as they reached for the same bread roll, the way they leaned closer, as though the private cabin wasn't intimate enough. It was the way their laughter filled the space like music, creating a melody even the jet's engines seemed to hum along to. As the second course arrived, a grilled lobster tail with tropical mango salsa and coconut rice, the plane flew into the heart of the night. Outside, the stars shone brighter, glowing as though offering their blessings to the happy couple. The flight attendant dimmed the lights further, leaving the glow of only the candles and the stars to light their evening. Dessert was decadent yet playful: a plate of tropical fruit sorbet served alongside a chocolate cake, dusted with powdered sugar. The flight attendant placed it on the table with a small pot of coffee.

They exchanged a look, their smiles so full of love that words were unnecessary. Taylor leaned over to remove a tiny piece of chocolate cake from Naomi's lips with his mouth.

"You know," he said, his voice low, "I'd fly to the ends of the earth if it meant I could spend just one more minute like this with you."

Naomi blushed at his words as they enjoyed the last of their dessert.

The cabin fell silent, except for the distant hum of the engines and the rhythmic beating of their hearts. As Taylor leaned in for a kiss, Fiji grew closer, not just in miles, but in the dreams they carried for their future together.

The cabin a blend of modern sophistication and timeless elegance, transformed into a serene bedroom at 40,000 feet. As the evening deepened, the flight attendant, with a discreet nod, initiated the transformation. Seats that once faced each other for intimate conversations now parted, reclining into a sumptuous bed. The walls of the cabin contained hidden sliding panels, creating a private sanctuary in the sky.

The bed was adorned with a plush, down-filled comforter and pillows that promised a restful slumber. The linens, a crisp, snowy white, were accented with throws and cushions in soft, muted tones. A collection of ambient lights above mimicked the star-studded sky outside, their gentle glow a lullaby for the senses. Naomi had never experienced such pampering, Taylor truly upped his game significantly. They'd flown together on a private jet before, but never overnight.

Naomi, her eyes reflecting the stars above, slipped underneath the covers, the silk of her gown whispering against the sheets. Taylor joined Naomi, wrapping his arms around her. He adored his wife and enjoyed every part of her body. The hum of the engines was a distant melody, concealing their night of passion.

As they settled in for the remainder of the flight, the flight attendant offered a finishing touch of hospitality, a carafe of warm spiced milk and a plate of delicate pastries. With a soft "goodnight," the attendant retreated, leaving the couple to their dreams. Naomi picked up one of the pastries offering Taylor the first bite.

"Very tasty," he smiled, licking her fingertips.

"Is it good?" Naomi asked.

"Not as delicious as you," Taylor winked.

She playfully slapped his arm, blushing as she sampled a pastry.

"I have never had spiced milk before," Naomi said, taking a long sip. "Oh, that's wonderful, reminds me of a chai latte."

He shared the remainder of the pastries with Naomi as they connected on a deeper level. There, above the clouds, Taylor and Naomi found peace unattainable on the ground. The jet carried them not just toward their destination, but through the realms of sleep and desire, where the only reality was their love and the murmur of the night wind against the jet's body.

Their peaceful sleep was interrupted briefly by the voice of the pilot announcing they would be landing in Fiji within the next two hours. The aroma of breakfast being prepared stirred them completely out of their slumber. Moments later the flight attendant quietly slipped in a tray of hot breakfast for the couple to enjoy. Naomi stretched her arms wide in preparation for her adventure. She was so content at this moment, turning to her husband with a broad smile. And as if Taylor read her mind, he pulled her body to his for a last-minute mid-air tryst.

"This breakfast stayed pretty warm considering," Taylor winked.

"I am too excited to eat," Naomi smiled, leaving her plate virtually untouched.

The couple showered and dressed preparing for their arrival. Inside the jet, Naomi and Taylor felt a mix of excitement and anticipation. The small cabin crew appeared and moved with practiced elegance, ensuring that every detail was perfect for the couple. As the jet approached the runway, the gentle hum of the engines was the only sound that filled the cabin.

The plane's landing gear touched down smoothly on the tarmac, the tires brushing the ground with a soft thud. The jet taxied to a halt and the door opened to reveal a world of vibrant colors and intoxicating fragrances. Palm trees swayed gently in the breeze, their branches whispering secrets of paradise. The air was fragrant with the scent of tropical flowers, mingling with the salty tang of the ocean.

A welcoming committee awaited them, their smiles as warm as the sun above. The sound of traditional Fijian music drifted through the air, carried by the voices of the singers and the rhythmic beat of the drums. Garlands of fragrant flowers were draped around the necks of the couple, a symbol of hospitality and friendship. Naomi's eyes sparkled with unshed tears of happiness. Taylor squeezed her hand, his heart bulging with love and the promise of the days to come.

The Fijian sun hung low in the sky, bathing the island in a golden hue, as if the very heavens were celebrating their arrival. In this moment, on the threshold of their new life together, Taylor and Naomi knew that every dream they'd ever had for their honeymoon was about to come true. Fiji was a paradise of islands where the peacock blue sea meets endless skies. Naomi and Taylor traveled to one of the more private islands Fiji offered, Royal Davui Island. Their day began with the sun casting a golden glow over the white sandy beaches, and they spent their morning snorkeling in the clear lagoons, discovering vibrant coral reefs teeming with marine life.

Naomi and Taylor walked hand in hand casually dressed, taking on the local vibes. As evening fell, they retreated to their private villa, a traditional Fijian cottage with modern amenities, where they were serenaded by the gentle sounds of the waves. They enjoyed light refreshments that were waiting for them inside. Their villa was perched on stilts above the crystal-clear waters which was a haven of harmony and romance. The walls were adorned with local art, telling stories of the island's rich culture and heritage. The resort's tranquility and privacy allowed them to connect on a deeper level, sharing stories and dreams and making love under the glowing sky.

The sun dipped below the horizon, painting the sky in hues of fiery orange and soft lavender. The gentle lapping of the waves against the white sandy shore played a soothing melody, as the scent of tropical flowers filled the air. It was the first evening of Naomi and Taylor's honeymoon in Fiji, and the world seemed to stand still in honor of their love.

The next morning, they enjoyed an early beach breakfast and as they walked hand in hand along the beach, the cool sand squishing between their toes, Naomi couldn't help but feel a sense of serenity wash over her. The stress of the wedding planning and the long flight faded away, leaving only the joy of the present moment.

Taylor, ever the romantic, had planned a surprise for their dinner. A private table was set up under a canopy of stars, with a path of flickering torches leading the way. The table was decorated with a bouquet of exotic flowers, their fragrance a pleasant treat to their nostrils. The gentle glow of tiny candles created an intimate atmosphere.

Their meal was a feast for the senses, a fusion of local flavors and international cuisine. Each course was a delightful surprise, from the fresh seafood to the decadent dessert, paired perfectly with a bottle of red wine. Taylor decided to skip his usual whisky while he traveled. As they dined, they shared stories of their adventures, dreams for the future, and laughter that echoed into the night. The connection between them was palpable, a bond strengthened by the shared experience of this enchanting place.

After dinner, they strolled back to their villa, where the night was still young. The private outdoor shower beckoned, promising a refreshing end to the warm evening. With a simple gesture, Taylor pointed at the shower door, inviting his bride to accompany him. With a mischievous grin, Taylor turned on the shower and a refreshing spray of water rushed forth, sparkling in the moonlight. Naomi let out an enjoyable laugh, her eyes radiating with excitement. Naomi smiled, taking Taylor's outstretched hand. They assisted one another by playfully removing each other's clothes.

"Come on," she said, running into the shower first, mischievously splashing water at him. "I bet you can't catch me!"

"Challenge accepted," he smiled.

Taylor joined her under the cool water, the droplets creating a shimmering curtain around them. They laughed and teased each other, their playful banter echoing through the late evening. The water flowed over their rich brown skin, washing away the remnants of sand from their beachside escapade. As they moved closer, Naomi reached for a bottle of fragrant coconut body wash and a large natural sea sponge. With a loving touch she pulled Taylor's head toward her as she began to lather his hair, her fingers massaging his scalp. She then used the sponge to wash his muscular frame in circular motions up and down his body. He closed his eyes, savoring every sensation. Taylor turned his body slightly so Naomi could wash his back.

In return, he took the soap and sponge and softly rubbed it over her shoulders first, working his way down her petite frame, his touch tender and caring. Taylor's broad body seemed to tower over her more than usual, but he was always gentle with her despite his size.

Their laughter turned into soft whispers and sensuous kisses, the intimacy of the moment deepening their bond. The shower became a sanctuary, a place where they could revel in their love and the simple joy of being together. The couple finally stepped out of the shower, wrapping in plush towels. Taylor effortlessly picked Naomi up as they shared a contented smile, knowing that this playful, carefree moment would be one of the many cherished memories from their honeymoon. He carried his bride to their villa where they enjoyed a sampling of wines.

"Are you trying to get me tipsy?" Naomi laughed.

"Is it working?" Taylor quipped.

Her laughter was infectious, he enjoyed her company immensely. Taylor sat fascinated that he was married to Naomi. He marveled at the depth of his feelings for her, emotions he had never experienced with such intensity before. He recalled the way she had held his hand during their first dance, her touch both gentle and firm, as if to say she would never let go. The laughter they shared during the reception, surrounded by family and friends was a testament to the happiness they had found in each other. He felt a sense of awe and gratitude that someone so incredible had chosen to share her life with him.

"What are you thinking about?" Naomi asked, stirring him from his trance.

"I am thinking that I am the luckiest man alive," he said, sincerely.

"Then that must make me the luckiest woman," she said.

Taylor stared through to her soul, which caused Naomi to feel so vulnerable but secure in his presence. The same butterflies she felt when they first kissed were fluttering fiercely on the inside of her. He pulled her close to him, slowly stroking her hair as he lovingly kissed her soft lips. Later, they retreated to the comfort of their bed, exploring each other's body as if for the first time until the gentle rocking of the water beneath them lulled them into a peaceful sleep.

The night was filled with the sounds of the island, a symphony of nature that serenaded them throughout their dreams. Taylor held Naomi close while the two of them slept.

Each of their mornings were spent sampling a variety of freshly prepared delicate pastries and succulent fruits. Their afternoons were filled with adventure; they explored the lush tropical gardens, finding hidden spots under the shade of the towering coconut palm trees on Royal Davui Island, stealing passionate kisses in paradise. Naomi and Taylor indulged in the local cuisine of rice, sweet potatoes, fish, and coconut, along with tropical and juicy, delectable fruits, with flavors as rich and colorful as the Fijian culture, enjoying private beachfront dinners as the sunset painted the sky in hues of orange and pink.

In Fiji, they found more than just a beautiful destination; they found a deeper connection to each other and a renewed sense of wonder. It was the beginning of their journey as husband and wife, a chapter of their story that they would cherish forever. Their honeymoon was a blend of relaxation and excitement, with each day bringing a new discovery on the island that spoke of love. A week of romance and solace ended as they headed to the airport for their return home.

Chapter 4

Monday morning ended their two-week fairytale as the sun peeked through the bedroom curtains greeting Naomi and Taylor with its warmth. Still locked in Taylor's tender embrace, she stirred first, waking him from a deep sleep.

"Do we have to go into the agency today?" Taylor said, stretching his arms.

"I am afraid so, but I will give you an extra hour," she said, snuggling back into his arms.

Taylor happily complied with her request without hesitation using the entire hour he was allowed.

They enjoyed a light breakfast of pastries and coffee before leaving for the agency, taking one car for the first time. The conversation was all business switching gears from their breakfast chat. The first order of business would be to select the agency's new name. Naomi had several ideas to consider, and they debated over allowing input from the original staff of Margaret and Sheila.

"The two I really like are 'Secure Justice' or 'Elite Justice,'" Taylor offered.

"Hmmm those are really good Mr. Sylvester," Naomi smiled.

"We can put them to a vote once we get to the office and I will order new signage for our offices," he said.

"You are the best partner," Naomi said, winking at him.

They arrived at the agency welcomed by a festive '**Congratulations Newlyweds**' banner and warm embraces all around. Margaret Regis led the way with an armload of gifts as well as mail and a stack of files.

"Welcome back both of you, I hope you are well rested and ready to work. Sheila and I have handled most of the cases that came through the office, but I have several clients that have requested you personally Naomi," Margaret told her. The two were on a first-named basis now after their rocky start last year.

"Looks like there is no rest for the weary," Naomi laughed, following Margaret as she entered her office.

Margaret placed the stack of folders neatly on the awaiting desk Naomi cleared off prior to her extended leave. Taylor on the other hand brushed passed Naomi on the way to his office.

"And where do you think you are going Mr. Sylvester," Margaret chastised, stopping him in his tracks.

"I'm just getting out of the way so the two of you can get down to business," Taylor quickly responded.

"I have mail and a stack of legal cases for you as well," she informed him sternly.

"No rest for the weary indeed," he said, shaking his head.

Secure Justice Agency was the unanimously agreed upon agency name and with that the day was filled with catching up on the previous weeks' happening and sorting through potential new cases. There were several promising cases, most of which Naomi felt could be easily handled without much effort, the clients only requested her by name because of her track record. She could assign another agent but would handle the preliminary interviews to put her personal touch on each one.

The last folder she picked up was marked '**Confidential-For Naomi Bloom's Eyes Only.**' Naomi was intrigued as she carefully opened the folder. She was shocked to see the name of the client inside was Cassandra Collins. Cassandra and Naomi had lost touch after Naomi uncovered her infidelity. Cassandra was embarrassed to the point where she had changed her telephone number. Naomi read the case file in disbelief; her one-time friend was being accused of murdering a man that she met once at a convention in San Diego and was in jail in Texas, where Cassandra and her family moved to in an attempt to get a fresh start.

Apparently, the man had continued to attempt to extort her even after she confessed to her husband. The encounter with the man caused her to lose her job at the bank and his incessant calls forced them to relocate. The man, whose name was Sebastian Daniels, was found dead in his hotel room and Cassandra was the last person to see him alive. Naomi had a flashback to DC and the betrayal she endured from someone she previously knew and trusted. Did she want to get caught up in something like this again? Lies and deceit troubled her, but she had a new sense of discernment.

She decided to share the information with Taylor to get his opinion. Naomi entered Taylor's office quietly since he was on a conference call with a client. She sat down slowly onto the leather couch in his office, patiently waiting for the call to end. Taylor looked up to acknowledge her presence as he wrapped up the conversation.

"I will be able to fit you in this week," Taylor told the caller.

With that the call ended and he stood from his desk to join Naomi on the sofa.

"You look troubled," Taylor told her, as he sat down.

"I have something to show you," she said, handing him the folder.

Taylor opened the folder and quickly reviewed the contents. Naomi never informed Taylor about Cassandra's infidelity, since this was her truth to tell.

"So, this is why the two of you don't speak anymore?" he asked with a concerned look.

"Yes, I thought Cassandra was connected to the Debugger case because she was acting very strange one day and never shared with me and I did not press her about it, but I later found explicit pictures of her with another man," Naomi explained.

"Wow, Naomi I am sorry about that, do you plan to help her?" Taylor asked.

"That's why I am in here, what do you think I should do? Just reading the file brought back difficult memories for me," Naomi confided.

"We can handle it together if you want. Sounds like she needs some legal advice as well," Taylor offered.

Naomi hugged Taylor, appreciating his understanding and support. The Secure Justice Detective Agency had its first case under its new name. Naomi and Taylor agreed to handle it from a two-pronged approach. Naomi wanted to make sure she did her due diligence before traveling to meet with her new client, Cassandra Collins. Naomi started out by requesting a complete background search on Sebastian Daniels to find out who he was. The more information she could find the better she would be able to help Cassandra.

Naomi was not having much luck with information on Daniels which was an instant red flag for Naomi. Her intuition was set ablaze, and she knew there was more to uncover about Sebastian Daniels. Taylor looked into the nuances of Texas law to assist with her situation. Cassandra currently had a public defender who was sloppy at best with her case. She was not formally charged but her public defender bungled her paperwork to get bail. Taylor contacted a former colleague at a Dallas law firm who was waiting to assist them if needed.

Since Texas does have automatic discovery, Cassandra would have to request whatever added information or evidence Naomi uncovered.

The Dallas police department felt they had an open and shut case against Cassandra so for them the investigation was closed. Naomi wanted to do right by her former friend whose dreams were shattered by one indiscretion. They were up against the clock. Naomi thought secretly that she owed it to Cassandra by not mentioning the affair to her when she first discovered the photos, maybe her old friend would not be in this position had she said something. Naomi could not dwell on the past or what ifs, she had to move forward.

"What do you say we call it an early day," Taylor suggested. "This has already been a lot to take in for one day."

"Come to mention it, I am a little worn down from traveling," she confessed.

Armed with the little information they could find, Naomi instructed Margaret to make travel arrangements to Dallas for Wednesday morning, allowing time for any remaining information to be uncovered. Naomi made a checklist of what she needed to get accomplished before their trip.

"Margaret, Taylor and I are going to head out for the rest of the day," Naomi said over the speakerphone.

Taylor whisked his bride off to a late lunch at one of his favorite restaurants. He had reservations for the two of them.

"Something tells me this was your plan all along Mr. Sylvester," she scolded.

"I tried to get you to stay home," He smirked.

Naomi did not mind the break, it was a bit overwhelming that their first case back would be something from her past she wanted to stay buried, but Taylor was the expert at knowing exactly what she needed at all times. The food was delicious, and his company was the perfect pairing.

"Did we leave room for dessert?" The waitress asked the couple.

Naomi smiled, "Only if you have bread pudding."

"Make that two, she does not like to share," Taylor laughed, checking his watch.

"This is the second time you've looked at your watch," Naomi commented.

"Just a bad habit," he fibbed, timing the second part of his plan.

The waitress returned with two freshly baked pieces of bread pudding drizzled with a rum sauce and paired with a single scoop of ice cream. The decadent masterpiece was a delightful sight. The texture was a symphony of contrasts; the top layer was a golden brown, baked to perfection, giving way to a lusciously soft custardy center that captured their senses. They playfully fed one another from opposite plates. Each bite was a montage of flavors, with the warm, buttery essence of the pudding combining harmoniously with the deep complex sweetness of the rum sauce, which was a masterpiece of its own. It was drizzled generously over the soft bread. Its velvety texture was a cascade of flavors with hints of vanilla, cinnamon, and caramel carefully blended with the punch of the rum.

The sauce seeped through each layer of the bread pudding, so each spoonful was a boozy delight on their palate. With each bite Naomi fed Taylor, she slid her spoon through the creamy sauce, then followed it with a spoonful of homemade vanilla ice cream. Once dessert was finished, the blushing waitress returned for their plates and handed Taylor a black folio with their bill. Taylor quickly slipped $300 inside without looking at the bill and handed it back to the waitress.

"Keep the change," he told the waitress.

"I think that was the best bread pudding I have ever eaten," Naomi smiled brightly.

"Let's head home," Taylor said, escorting her from the table.

When they arrived home, Naomi headed straight for the shower to unwind for the rest of the evening.

The delivery Taylor was waiting for arrived just as Naomi turned off the water to the shower. Taylor could hear her upstairs as she performed her after shower ritual. He knew it would take her fifteen minutes before coming downstairs, time enough for him to get everything in place. He poured her a glass of wine and himself a glass of whiskey and returned to the den. He arranged an assortment of her favorite books on the coffee table and sat down with a magazine, just as Naomi stepped in the room.

"You look mighty comfy Mr. Sylvester, may I join you?" she asked.

Taylor smiled and motioned for her to come sit next to him. Naomi picked up one of the books, snuggled beside him and sipped on wine as she read. He waited until both their glasses were empty, then excused himself to refresh their drinks.

As the sun dipped below the horizon, casting a warm glow over the newlyweds' cozy den, Taylor tiptoed behind Naomi, who was curled up on the couch, lost in her book. The air was filled with the comforting scent of vanilla from the candles flickering softly on the mantelpiece.

"Close your eyes baby and hold out your arms," Taylor whispered, his voice tinged with excitement.

Naomi looked up, her eyes sparkling with curiosity, and obliged, a smile playing on her lips.

Taylor carefully placed a small, wiggling bundle in her outstretched arms.

"Now, open them," he said.

Naomi's eyes fluttered open, and she gasped. In her arms was a jet black French Bulldog puppy, its tiny body wiggling furiously. The puppy's bright eyes looked up at her, full of affection and playfulness. She noticed one eye was black and the other golden amber.

"Oh, Taylor!" Naomi exclaimed, her heart swelling with joy, "He's perfect!"

The puppy yipped and nuzzled into her neck, and Naomi laughed, a sound as clear and melodious as a bell. Taylor sat beside her, draping an arm around her shoulders.

"He's our first family addition," Taylor said proudly, his eyes gleaming with love. "I thought we could use a little more chaos around here."

Naomi leaned into Taylor, the puppy between them, feeling the warmth of her husband and the soft fur of the little creature that was already a part of their lives.

"I love you so much," she said, her voice soft but filled with emotion.

"I love you more," Taylor replied, and they both knew that their little family was just beginning.

"You have some tough competition now, you know how I love dogs," she smiled.

"I am sorry about the timing with the case, but he was already picked out for you when we returned from Fiji," he shared.

"I don't care, this is the best gift. He is so handsome," she laughed, nuzzling the puppy under her chin.

"What are you going to name him?" Taylor asked her.

"Let's name him Saint," she said.

"Saint it is," Taylor agreed. "I also arranged for the breeder to keep him while we are out of town, that's why I kept checking my watch," he shared.

Naomi placed Saint gently on the floor as they watched their new French Bulldog puppy clumsily navigate the soft carpet. The puppy, with its bat-like ears and smushed face, explored his new surroundings with innocent curiosity. Every now and then, he stopped to look up at his new owners, tiny tail wagging in a blur of excitement. Naomi and Taylor exchanged loving glances, their laughter mingling with the puppy's playful yelps. They raised a toast to their new furry family member, feeling a sense of completeness in their home.

Naomi gathered Saint's tiny bed and blanket in one hand as she tucked him in the other and headed upstairs.

"Have I relinquished my cuddle time to this little guy?" Taylor joked.

"Follow us and see," she smiled.

Taylor eagerly followed the two of them upstairs with haste. Naomi laughed hearing Taylor playfully pant behind her up the stairs, followed by a deep bark. Naomi appreciated the light-hearted fun because in a couple days they were stepping into the unknown.

Naomi packed their bags for their Wednesday trip as Taylor played with Saint. Taylor sat with his legs crossed, and in the cradle of his lap, the 6-week-old French Bulldog puppy tumbled about with youthful exuberance. Saint playfully nipped at Taylor's fingers, each bite, a gentle whisper against his skin. Taylor's laughter was a low, enjoyable rumble, a sound that seemed to resonate through their bedroom. His eyes were alight with a fondness that only a new pet owner knew, a mix of adoration and the quiet awe of companionship just beginning. Across the room, as she continued packing, Naomi leaned against the doorframe, stopping to watch the playful scene. Her arms were folded, a soft smile playing on her lips, her eyes reflecting the warmth that filled the space between the walls of their home.

"Time for Saint to go to bed, we have an early morning," Naomi said, interrupting their playtime.

"Yes ma'am, is it my bedtime too?" Taylor asked, sitting at attention.

"I have other plans for you Mr. Sylvester," Naomi said.

As the morning light filtered through the sheer curtains, casting a gentle glow across the room, Naomi stood by the bathroom door, her hand resting on the doorknob. She took a deep breath, her gaze lingering on the small, slumbering form of her French Bulldog puppy, Saint, nestled in his new bed. Taylor stepped from the shower as Naomi finished dressing.

"I almost hate to wake him," Naomi said kneeling to pick up Saint.

"He doesn't have a care in the world," Taylor laughed.

"Time to go for a ride," she whispered.

A protective instinct surged within her, making her second-guess leaving him so soon.

"He'll be just fine with the breeder, and he needs the rest of his shots," Taylor informed her.

"How long will he need to stay?" She asked, concerned.

"Since we will be traveling tomorrow, I arranged for him to stay until we get back," Taylor explained.

Naomi was hesitant to relinquish her puppy so soon, but it had to be done for his health. Taylor and Naomi headed into the office once they dropped Saint at the breeder.

Chapter 5

Naomi rubbed her temples as she read through the notes her team had gathered. Naomi stared at the glaring whiteboard in her meticulous office. The name "Sebastian Daniels" was scrawled in bold black letters at the center, surrounded by a web of notes, photos, and timelines. Naomi's jaw tightened as her eyes flicked to the photo of her friend, Cassandra Collins. Cassandra was in custody, accused of killing Sebastian Daniels. The evidence seemed airtight: she had been seen on security footage entering the hotel minutes before Sebastian Daniels's murder, her fingerprints were on the knife, and she had plenty of motive—Sebastian Daniels had been blackmailing her over something that could destroy her family, career, and reputation. But Naomi knew Cassandra, and she would bet everything she had that Cassandra was no killer. She was determined to find answers to all of the questions swirling through her mind.

As the Boeing 737 descended through the clouds, the vast expanse of Dallas stretched out below like an expansive tapestry. The sun was just beginning to peek above the horizon, casting a golden glow over the city. Inside their first-class cabin, passengers prepared for landing, stowing away their belongings and securing their seat belts. The flight was only an hour and twenty-five minutes, just enough time for a quick cup of coffee. Taylor peered out of the large oval window as the plane touched down with a gentle rumble at Dallas-Fort Worth International Airport, the gateway to a city where business and ambition thrived.

Taylor and Naomi gathered their belongings once the fasten seatbelt sign was turned off. Inside the terminal, the atmosphere buzzed with a blend of languages and the soft clacking of suitcase wheels. Business travelers navigated the concourse with practiced ease. Travelers hurried past Naomi and Taylor, some dragging suitcases behind them, others cradling sleepy children. The intercom chimed with announcements, and the scent of freshly brewed coffee wafted from a nearby cafe.

Taylor scanned the terminal for the familiar signs leading to the baggage claim. The digital screens overhead flickered with flight information, a symphony of arrivals and departures that mirrored the city's dynamic pulse. The baggage carousel churned out suitcases in a rhythmic cadence, and Taylor retrieved a sleek, black garment bag, waiting for another cycle to retrieve

Naomi's suitcase. They quickly headed to the exit to meet their limousine driver.

Outside, the Texas heat surrounded them like a warm embrace. A black sedan pulled up to the curb, its driver holding a sign with Sylvester on it. The car door opened, and Naomi and Taylor settled into the plush leather seats. As the car merged onto the highway, the city's skyline loomed ahead. The Ritz-Carlton was their final destination where they would reside while working on Cassandra's case.

"Can you recommend a good lunch spot?" Taylor asked the driver, as they got out of the car.

"Sure Mr. Sylvester, coming from New Orleans, you may want to try Antoine's Cajun Bistro, it has a wide selection of similar food you may enjoy. The driver assisted Naomi with her luggage as Taylor stepped inside the hotel.

Their hotel suite would not be ready until 1pm so they asked the driver to give them a tour around the city to kill time before taking them to the recommended restaurant for an early lunch. They took a slow drive through downtown Dallas, navigating a labyrinth of innovation connected with history. The city's skyline was an outline of towering skyscrapers, reflecting the golden tones of the bright morning sun, producing shadows over the bustling streets below. The iconic Reunion Tower punctuated the cityscape, its geodesic dome glittering like a morning star.

The vibration of the city was palpable as they drove past the historic Sixth Floor Museum at Dealey Plaza, where echoes of the past linger in the air. The vibrant Arts District beckoned with its cultural allure, home to the Dallas Museum of Art and the Winspear Opera House, their contemporary designs, a stark contrast to the red-brick charm of the West End Historic District. Once the tour was completed, the limousine driver transported Naomi and Taylor to the restaurant for an early lunch. He waited for them to finish their lunch to take them back to the hotel.

Their hotel room on the fifteenth floor was a sanctuary of luxury. The king-sized bed promised restful nights, and the view of the Dallas skyline. Naomi unpacked her luggage, organizing her clothes neatly in the closet. Taylor set up the laptop computer and hung his garment bag in the closet so his suits would not be wrinkled. It was time to get down to business, as he had several calls to make.

Naomi had never been to Dallas before, but she had a contact with the New Orleans police department who put her in communication with a police officer who would assist her with Cassandra's case. Prior to their arrival, Naomi requested a copy of the full crime scene report which was being sent to their hotel by courier. She had only received preliminary information and needed to have the big picture

At 2:30 PM the courier delivered the documents Naomi had requested. Naomi and Taylor reviewed the crime scene report which included photos of Sebastian Daniels' dead body. He had been strangled and stabbed multiple times. Per the police report he put up quite a struggle before he died.

"How can a woman overpower a man and do this much damage?" Naomi said, pointing to the graphic photos.

"Well, I have seen Cassandra in person on a few occasions and I don't see it happening," Taylor agreed.

Based on that bit of information alone Naomi wanted to speak with Cassandra in person. She also scheduled an appointment with Cassandra's public defender. Taylor contacted his attorney colleague, and they were meeting at his law firm at 3:00 PM so he headed to his office and would meet Naomi at the jail to see Cassandra.

The heavy door clanged shut behind Naomi, the sound echoing off the stark concrete walls. She stood in the visiting area of the city jail, a place that reeked of despair and bleach. It was a stark contrast to the vibrant energy she was used to in her line of work as a private investigator. She approached the glass partition, her heart pounding with a mixture of dread and determination. Across from her, separated by a thick pane of glass, was Cassandra, her old friend, clad in an orange jumpsuit that seemed too large for her frame. They had been close at one time, two women meeting by chance years ago. But that was before the secret, before the day that changed everything. Now Cassandra was accused of a crime Naomi knew she couldn't have committed. Her face was dim, the usual spark in her eyes Naomi remembered darkened by the fluorescent lights that hung above.

Minutes ticked by, filled with the echoes of distant conversations and the shuffling of feet. Naomi's heart raced as she searched for the right words. The secret lay between them, an invisible barrier as tangible as the glass between them.

"Hey, Cassandra," Naomi said, her voice barely a whisper.

The phone on her side of the glass felt cold and foreign in her hand. Cassandra picked up the receiver. Her eyes, once so full of life and laughter, were now dull and guarded.

"Naomi," Cassandra said, her voice barely above a whisper. "I didn't think you'd come."

"How could I not?" Naomi replied, her voice was steady, despite the turmoil inside her. "You're my friend, and you're innocent. I'm going to prove it."

"You still think of me as a friend?" Cassandra said, taken aback.

Naomi nodded her head, suppressing her hurt feelings.

They talked about the case, about the evidence Naomi had been gathering on the outside. Naomi detailed a few leads, shared some theories, and asked about Cassandra's alibi during the time of the murder. Cassandra listened, hope flickering in her eyes for the first time since her arrest.

"I never thought I'd see you here," Naomi finally said.

Cassandra's lips twisted into a bitter smile. "Nor did I."

Naomi's gaze dropped to the table.

"I'm sorry, Cassandra. I should've told you I found the pictures when we left your office," Naomi said.

"Stop," Cassandra cut her off, her voice sharp. "Just stop. It's done. What's the point of digging it all up now? It is not your fault. I should have told you what happened," Cassandra said.

"What happened Cassandra? I know I was caught up with my first case!" Naomi's voice rose, a note of desperation creeping in.

"You're sitting here because of me, because of what I didn't do that day. I saw the pictures and the note," She confessed to Cassandra.

Cassandra leaned back in her chair, the lines of her face contorting into shame.

"I made the mistake of trusting a stranger and that hurt my family and our friendship," Cassandra began.

Naomi's eyes met Cassandra's, searching for a sign of the friend she once knew.

"Why didn't you just tell me about the affair?" Naomi questioned.

A long silence stretched between them, filled with regret and unspoken apologies.

"Because it wasn't an affair," Cassandra said finally, her voice low. "I wanted to tell you everything. I didn't think you would ever want to see me again. I am so thankful you came,"

Naomi nodded her head slowly, a lump forming in her throat. The secret that caused them to lose their friendship now had her in jail. They would face it together. As the guard announced the end of visiting hours, Naomi stood up, placing her hand against the glass. Cassandra mirrored her movement, their palms lining up, a connection in their separation.

"I'll be back with more help if you are willing to accept it," Naomi promised.

"Yes, I'll be willing to accept," Cassandra replied, a faint glimmer of hope in her eyes.

Naomi lingered behind as she watched her friend, broken and defeated vanish behind a metal door which slammed behind her.

"I should've been there for her. I saw the signs, the distress in her eyes, but I... I just didn't realize," Naomi muttered to herself. "I can't change the past, but I'm here now. We will fight this together. I won't let Cassandra face this alone anymore," she told herself.

And with that, the two friends began the long journey of reconciliation. Naomi walked out of the jail, the image of Cassandra's hopeful gaze etched into her memory. Naomi wouldn't rest until she had uncovered the truth, and her friend was free. The case had just become personal.

Jonathan Walker agreed to meet Taylor at short notice due to the nature of the case. In his dimly lit confines of his downtown office, the two defense attorneys sat across from each other, their expressions subdued as they pored over the multitude of evidence sprawled before them. The bookcases were lined with legal books, the air thick with the weight of the case at hand. Jonathan, a seasoned lawyer with a reputation for his unorthodox methods, leaned back in his chair, his fingers tented in deliberation.

"The prosecution's case is circumstantial at best," Jonathan mused, his eyes scanning the autopsy report. "Your client may have been in a relationship with the victim, but that doesn't make her a murderer."

Taylor nodded in agreement. His swift analytical mind had already dissected every witness statement, every piece of forensic data.

"It's all about the narrative," Taylor said, tapping a photo of the crime scene. "Would you be willing to take her case? She has a weak ass public defender right now. It would mean a lot to Naomi."

"We need to construct a narrative that casts doubt, one that the judge or jury can believe if it goes to trial," Jonathan said, seemingly agreeing to take her case.

They both knew the stakes were high. An innocent woman's life hung in the balance, and the court of public opinion had already delivered its verdict. But in this room, facts were their currency, and they were about to make a compelling argument for the defense. Jonathan would accompany Taylor to meet Cassandra and hear her side of the story firsthand.

Taylor and Jonathan Walker met with Marc Xavier, Cassandra Collins' public defender. He was overworked and disinterested in her case. It was clear with their conversation that his lack of effort caused Cassandra to lose hope. Mr. Xavier was well aware of Jonathan Walker and his track record as a defense attorney. He was a no-nonsense attorney and a prosecutor's worst nightmare.

"Mr. Xavier, I am not here to step on your toes, but I have reviewed Mrs. Collins' case and feel she may benefit from my services. Mr. Sylvester is a former colleague who brought her case to my attention. Mrs. Collins has also enlisted a private investigator," Jonathan explained.

"Why does she need a private investigator?" Mr. Xavier asked, looking perplexed.

"If you have to ask maybe you're not her best representative, I would advise you step aside unless you want her to decide. Are you willing to continue with her case?" Jonathan asked.

"One less headache for me I guess," Mr. Xavier said.

Inside the dimly lit jail visitation room, Cassandra sat nervously awaiting Naomi to return. Jonathan Walker had arranged for a private room. The room was sparse and cold, only a table and a few chairs. She sat helplessly in handcuffs with an armed police officer standing close by. A few minutes passed before Naomi entered accompanied by Taylor, Jonathan Walker, and Marc Xavier. Cassandra's eyes widened at the trio of men following behind Naomi, with one unfamiliar face among the three, she looked on nervously.

Jonathan Walker sat first, placing his briefcase on the table, "Cassandra, I'm Jonathan Walker. I'll be taking over your case from Mr. Xavier"

"Why? What's wrong with him?" Cassandra asked, with skepticism,

Mr. Xavier interjected, "Nothing's wrong. It's just that Mr. Walker has certain resources that I don't."

Jonathan, giving Mr. Xavier a stern look, "Let's just say, I believe everyone deserves a fair shot, and I'm here to ensure you get yours."

"Fair shot? I've been sitting in this cell for days because someone thinks I'm a criminal!" Cassandra said, defeat in her voice,

"I've reviewed your file, and I see a lot of inconsistencies and overlooked evidence. I'm here to fight for you, Cassandra. But I need you to tell me everything, no matter how insignificant it may seem."

"I've told Mr. Xavier everything already," Cassandra said with hesitation.

"With all due respect to Mr. Xavier, I'm not him. I have a different approach, and I promise you, I will leave no stone unturned," Jonathan assured her.

"Cassandra, I promised you I would help you and I intend to keep my word," Naomi reassured her.

Mr. Xavier nodded in agreement.

"He's the best, Cassandra. If anyone can get you out of this, it's him." Taylor chimed in.

"Alright. Where do we start?" Cassandra now had a glimmer of hope in her eyes.

"From the beginning, Cassandra. From the very beginning. And this time, we'll get it right," Jonathan told her.

Mr. Xavier excused himself from the visiting room, promising to hand over any documents he had in his possession pertaining to her case. Naomi squeezed Cassandra's hand as a sign of support for her friend. A single tear fell from Cassandra's eye as she started from the painful beginning. Cassandra's voice was shaky, nervous from embarrassment to retell her nightmare.

"I was at a banking convention in San Diego for my job when I first met Sebastian Daniels. He was at one of the breakout sessions with fellow bank managers. He was funny and seemed brilliant the way he spoke with confidence at our table," she said, eyes lowered as she spoke.

"We shared lunch as a group the first two days until he invited me to happy hour for drinks. It was an innocent conversation. We talked about our jobs and our families. He was interested in the investment side of banking and asked if I enjoyed what I did. Happy hour turned into dinner and then we went to lunch alone, still only discussing business," Cassandra continued.

"Thursday evening came along, and we met for happy hour again. I only had two drinks, but the second drink was more than I could handle. Sebastian had to help me back to my room and when I awoke the next morning I had the worst headache. My clothes were in a neat pile on the floor, I was in my underwear and my purse, and keys were next to the bed. I quickly showered, dressed, and headed to the last session of the convention. I looked for Sebastian to thank him for getting me to my room but could not find him. I only assumed he was late since he had more drinks than I had."

Jonathan took notes as Cassandra retold her account of what happened.

"I began to worry about what happened to Sebastian as the convention ended because he was a no show. At the conclusion of the convention, I checked with hotel concierge to discover he checked out of the hotel that morning."

Naomi looked on overly concerned because she knew now her friend was clearly taken advantage of.

"I returned home and thought nothing more of the encounter until a few weeks later when I received an envelope at work. When I opened the envelope, my world shook," she said nervously.

"Cassandra, why didn't you say something to me as soon as it happened?" Naomi asked, sorrowfully.

"Naomi you were occupied with your investigation. I did not want to bother you about my problems. You walked in on the second conversation I had with Sebastion. The first time he called I genuinely thought he was checking on me, but I was so wrong. He only wanted to make sure it was me before he told me what he did. He had gotten enough information from me before slipping something in my drink. I foolishly trusted a stranger and let my guard down. He threatened to blackmail me outright, but I refused and told him I would go to the police, then the pictures came with the note indicating we were in a relationship. I was ashamed and afraid." Cassandra said.

Naomi was shocked by what she was hearing. How could she be so wrong?

"Cassandra I must be honest, I thought you were involved in my case when you ran out of the restaurant crying during our lunch. You just said you were having a difficult day when I asked about it. You dropped the envelope with the pictures in your office and it was then I knew you had no involvement. I should have said something to you, but my investigation took an unexpected turn," Naomi confessed.

"It was my fault for not telling you and for my insensitivity to your concerns about Henry Williams. I allowed my problem to cause a strained friendship, and I am so sorry for missing your wedding," Cassandra sobbed.

"We can't change what happened Cassandra so let's put the past behind us and work on clearing your name," Naomi told her.

"I read the case file, and the police evidence is not strong enough to even hold you in jail, in my opinion. I will work on getting you bail," Jonathan told her.

"You mean I will get out of this horrible place?" she asked with uneasy excitement.

"Yes, you have no reason to leave the state, your husband and child are both here. I will stress that with the judge," Jonathan said.

"I cannot thank you enough for helping me Mr. Walker," Cassandra said, wiping tears from her face.

"We have much work to do, and it might become challenging, but I feel confident," Jonathan smiled.

It had been a long day, but Naomi had reason to be optimistic over what transpired. When they left the jail, ominous storm clouds overtook the sky. She and Taylor arrived back at the hotel before the rain started. They ordered room service in lieu of going out. The guilt she had felt earlier was symbolically washed away with the downpour outside. After a light dinner she wanted to take another look at the case file to see what she could have missed.

"Let's look at things with fresh eyes tomorrow," Taylor told her, taking the file from her hand, placing it on the desk.

"You're right," she told him, without any argument.

"We both had a long day. I think we owe ourselves a little downtime," Taylor said gently.

The rain tapped against the windowpane, a gentle rhythm that echoed the beat of their hearts. In their hotel bedroom, the scent of jasmine candles lingered—a reminder of their wedding night. Naomi sat on the edge of the bed, her fingers tracing the intricate pattern on the quilt. Her dark hair framed her face, she brushed her hair slowly as she prepared for bed.

Across the room, Taylor stood by the television looking for a music channel. He turned, catching Naomi's gaze, and crossed the room to join her.

"Remember our first dance?" Taylor asked, his voice a low murmur.

Naomi smiled; her eyes distantly remembering the moment. "At the Jazz festival. You stepped on my toes, and I pretended not to mind,"

He chuckled, taking her hand. "And remember that rainy afternoon when we kissed under an old oak tree?"

"The raindrops tasted like sweet promises," Naomi replied. "Promises we've kept."

Taylor pulled her closer, their bodies fitting together like pieces of a puzzle.

"We've weathered storms," he said. "Experienced exciting times, faced difficulties, but through it all, you've been my anchor."

Naomi rested her head against his chest, listening to the steady rhythm of his heartbeat.

"And you," she whispered, "have been my beacon—guiding me home."

They swayed to the soft music that played, their steps slow and deliberate. The rain outside intensified, a symphony of memories. Taylor's lips brushed against her forehead, then to her lips, and Naomi closed her eyes, savoring the taste of love.

"Will you dance with me forever?" Taylor asked.

Naomi nodded. "Through any obstacle, good times and bad. Let's never lose trust in one another. Our love will remain."

Taylor took his time pleasing his wife as the music continued to play softly as a background to their endless passion. He did not want them to lose that honeymoon feeling so soon. He was not ready to share his wife with work, knowing how focused Naomi could get. Taylor watched over Naomi as she slept, grateful for their relationship.

Jonathan was able to get a bond hearing for Cassandra the following afternoon. The courtroom was filled with a tense silence as Jonathan stood confidently in front of the judge, ready to present his case. Cassandra sat beside him with a mixture of hope and anxiety in her eyes.

"Your Honor, we are here today because justice demands that an innocent person should not spend a single unnecessary minute behind bars. My client, whom I stand beside, has been wrongfully accused, and it is our plea that she be granted bond while we prepare to clear her name," Jonathan said with assertion.

The judge, an older, stern-looking woman, peered over her glasses, scrutinizing the evidence, and looking in the direction of Jonathan Walker and Cassandra.

"I have reviewed the evidence presented before me, and I must say, it is rather thin. What assurances can you give this court that your client will not flee once released?" Judge Tenette asked.

Jonathan took a moment, then responded with unwavering certainty.

"Your Honor, my client has a steady job, and a family that depends on her. She has no prior record, and there is substantial evidence that we are prepared to present that will exonerate her of all charges. In fact, we will prove that she was a victim as well.

Judge Tenette nodded, taking in the information, then turned to the prosecutor, who had remained silent up to this point.

"Does the state have any objections to the defense's request for bond?" The judge asked.

The prosecutor stood slowly, his expression was unreadable.

"No, Your Honor. The state does not object," he concurred.

A murmur ran through the courtroom as the judge made a note, then she looked up, ready to deliver her decision.

"In light of the arguments presented and the lack of objection from the state, I am inclined to grant bond. The court hereby sets a bond at $50,000. The defendant is to surrender her passport and report to the bail officer weekly," Judge Tenette ordered.

Cassandra exhaled a sigh of relief, tears welling up in her eyes. Jonathan placed a reassuring hand on her shoulder, looking behind him at Naomi and Taylor.

Chapter 6

The body of Sebastian Daniels was not claimed by any relatives, so Naomi was able to pull a few strings to visit the morgue to view the body in person, there was something about the crime scene photos that did not make sense.

The morgue was a silent symphony of death's finality, a stark contrast to the chaos of the living world just beyond its walls. Stainless steel tables lined the room, each holding the last earthly remains of souls departed. The air was thick with the antiseptic stink of chemicals, a futile defense against the inevitable decay. The room was dimly lit, except for the harsh fluorescent beams spotlighting the cold metal slab in the center. There, a body lay covered by a thin, blue sheet, the stillness of death enveloping it like a shroud.

The medical examiner lifted the sheet, revealing the victim's face. "Sebastian Daniels," he said, "found stabbed to death in his hotel room."

Naomi carefully looked at his face, but it was not the same man from the photos she saw with Cassandra. She noticed the bruises on his arms where he struggled with his attacker before being overpowered.

"Who are you?" she asked aloud, half expecting him to answer her.

A chill ran down Naomi's spine. The pieces were not falling into place, nor forming the picture she wished for but instead remained incomplete. "Looks like the past isn't done with us me," she said, her eyes fixed on the lifeless form before her. "It's time to dig deeper."

As the medical examiner covered the body back, Naomi turned away, her resolve hardening. The morgue, a final resting place for some, was just the beginning for her. The hunt was on, and she would not rest until justice was served.

Naomi contacted Jonathan and asked to meet with him and Cassandra.

"Jonathan, I have some very interesting news that cannot wait"? Naomi said with excitement in her voice.

"I will call Cassandra immediately to set up the meeting," he told Naomi.

Taylor was waiting for Naomi in the car, and she filled him in on what she discovered.

"Let's head to Jonathan's office to get him caught up," Naomi told him.

The drive to Jonathan's office took them almost thirty minutes in traffic. Naomi's mind raced with the information she uncovered. Once they arrived, both Jonathan and Cassandra were anxiously waiting.

"Cassandra did the police show you a picture of Sebastian Daniels' body?" Naomi asked, holding the autopsy report.

"No, they didn't, and I am not sure I want to see it now," she said shaking her head.

"Why do you ask Naomi?" Jonathan interjected.

"Well first, if I was accused of murder, I would want to see the evidence and second, I would want to confirm who the victim is," Naomi smiled, sliding the report to Jonathan.

He carefully opened the folder then showed the picture to Cassandra. Cassandra's facial expression said what everyone one else was thinking. Who was this? The murder victim in the photo may have been identified as Sebastian Daniels but it was not the same Sebastian Daniels Cassandra met in San Diego.

"What is going on here Naomi? Who is this man?" Cassandra asked, in complete disbelief.

"That is the big mystery," Naomi said. "Why would you murder a complete stranger?"

"I must say, this case has me intrigued like none I have ever seen," Jonathan said.

"We have our work cut out for us," Taylor added.

Cassandra was temporarily relieved that she had a real chance of having the murder charges against her dropped until a chill ran through her realizing a murderer was on the loose.

"Naomi, I think we just need to turn this over to the police," Taylor told her, concerned.

"We need to get the charges against Cassandra dropped first. We came here to help her and that's what I intend to do," Naomi said.

Taylor knew his wife, that once her mind was made up, it would not be changed, especially if she was correct.

"I promise to be careful and keep you involved every step of the way," she assured him.

Cassandra explained to the trio that she received a call from Sebastian Daniels to meet him in the lobby of the Omni Hotel. She could not believe that he had found out that she had moved to Dallas. He had demanded $5,000 from her to make him destroy the original photos. To Cassandra it was worth the money because she had too much to lose. Ashamed, Cassandra had confessed to her husband what happened, and he was incredibly supportive because he could have easily lost his wife. She was forced to leave her job in New York because of the harassment. Her mistake was not changing her phone number.

"When I arrived at the hotel, I went to the reservation desk and asked for Sebastian Daniels," Cassandra said. "The hotel concierge told me they could not give out his room number, but they would call his room. I waited for a few minutes and then I saw someone who resembled him sitting in the lobby. I didn't even make eye contact, I just threw the envelope at his feet and left the hotel."

"Did he say anything to you?" Jonathan asked.

"I heard him saying wait," Cassandra told Jonathan. "I felt sick to my stomach, so I left."

"So that's how the police tied you to the murder" Taylor said.

Naomi was impressed with Taylor's deduction. Cassandra was a victim of a sick type of extortion scheme that turned into murder. Based on the evidence the police gathered from the hotel, an empty envelope and money in Sebastian Daniels' hotel room, eyewitnesses placed her at the scene and the concierge told the police she requested Mr. Daniels at the front desk. Whoever this person was he had to have known the victim.

"Why would someone want to do this to me?" Cassandra asked in disbelief.

"Unfortunately, there are some sick ass people in this world," Taylor said.

"First thing we need to do is get a copy of the hotel footage of the lobby because the police only have footage of you at the front desk," Naomi said.

"I will draft a motion to request the footage," Jonathan said.

SHATTERED DREAMS

Jonathan was able to have his motion granted to gain access to all hotel footage from the night Cassandra was at the hotel. He requested the new video be reviewed by his team in the presence of the Dallas police department as a show of good faith. Jonathan, Taylor, and Naomi met with Sergeant McLaughlin in one of the police department's interrogation rooms. He was accompanied by another police officer who was responsible for securing and playing the video. The new hotel footage began to roll, as Cassandra's legal team and the police watched as the timestamp in the corner ticked back to the night of the crime. The video, captured by security cameras in the lobby, showed Cassandra meeting with an unknown man, dropping an envelope, and then quickly exiting the hotel.

In the video, the man's face was shielded by a partition but there was another video from the front desk that showed 'Sebastian Daniels' checking out of the hotel, in clear view, was the figure of a man that Cassandra supposedly met with. The man in the video did not have the same features nor the same hair color as the man in her blackmail photos. And then, as if the world itself wanted to carve away any doubt, the man turned his face towards the camera, and it was not Daniels' face. A collective gasp rippled through the police interrogation room. The police sergeant sat back in his chair, his expression blank. Naomi and Taylor leaned forward; their eyes wide with the realization of what this meant.

The police officer let the video play to the end, then turned off the video player.

"Sergeant, the evidence is clear, based on the time stamp, my client Cassandra Collins was at home at the time of the murder, just as she has always claimed. And clearly the man in this video is not Mr. Sebastian Daniels," Jonathan concluded.

Sergeant McLaughlin nodded solemnly, his gaze shifting to Naomi and Taylor.

"Given this new evidence, I believe we have enough to drop all charges against Mrs. Collins."

Naomi squeezed Taylor's hand tightly, "I can't wait to tell Cassandra that this nightmare is almost over."

"Sergeant McLaughlin, we appreciate your assistance in the matter, but we have Detective Naomi Bloom to thank for figuring out what happened," Jonathan informed him.

"Miss Bloom thank you for your keen sense of awareness," Sergeant McLaughlin told her.

"It's Mrs. Sylvester actually, Bloom is my maiden name," Naomi smiled.

"Well Mrs. Sylvester, seems I still have a murderer to catch," Sergeant McLaughlin said disappointed.

"I suppose you do," she said.

"It's a bit unorthodox but would you be interested in helping us with this case since you figured out your client was innocent?" Sergeant McLaughlin asked her.

Naomi instinctively looked in Taylor's direction for approval. Her eyes quietly pleaded to continue with the investigation.

"Sergeant McLaughlin, my wife and I work as a team, as partners of Secure Justice Agency," Taylor clarified.

"The more eyes on this case, the better," McLaughlin told him.

Sergeant McLaughlin was a seasoned investigator with the Dallas Police Department. With over a decade of experience in law enforcement, McLaughlin had developed a reputation for his tenacity and sharp intuition. Born and raised in Texas, McLaughlin had always been drawn to the pursuit of justice. He graduated at the top of his class from the police academy and quickly rose through the ranks. Despite his small stature his tenacity and presence was giant. His associates admired him for his unwavering commitment and his ability to remain calm under pressure. McLaughlin appreciated another investigator that was as enthusiastic as him.

Naomi's eyes lit up with excitement since Taylor was in agreement with them continuing on with the investigation. She did not want to leave Dallas not knowing the outcome. This would also allow Naomi to go back home, when necessary, without feeling as if she were abandoning or ignoring Cassandra again.

Cassandra met with Sergeant McLaughlin accompanied by her attorney to formally discuss the video findings.

"Cassandra, we've reviewed the new evidence and It's clear you were at the wrong place at the wrong time," Sergeant McLaughlin told her.

"So, I... I am really free?" Cassandra looked up, stammering.

"Yes, but we need your help. You've had an interaction with the real perpetrator, and your testimony could make all the difference," Sergeant McLauglin said, affirming her question.

"If I do this..., will it be safe?" Cassandra asked looking concerned.

"We'll protect you and your family. Witness protection, if necessary. But without your help, we can't guarantee we'll catch who's really responsible," Sergeant McLauglin said earnestly.

Cassandra took a deep breath, looked at Jonathan, then steadied herself before speaking.

"Okay. I'll do it. I'll testify once you catch him."

Sergeant McLaughlin extended his hand, and Cassandra took it, their handshake sealing the newfound alliance. Jonathan shook hands with the Sergeant as well, securing a necessary asset in the police department. Cassandra exited the police station with fear and anticipation, her life had been in limbo for far too long. She rode back to the office with Jonathan to finalize her case and sign any necessary paperwork. On the car ride back, her cell phone rang. Cassandra answered the phone quickly.

"Hi honey," Cassandra answered cheerfully, assuming it was her husband, Charles.

"Hi sweetheart," the voice on the other end answered.

The color drained from Cassandra's face as the phone dropped from her hand. Jonathan looked at her concerned, tears dropping from her eyes. He picked up the phone only to hear a voice at the other end calling her name over and over again. Jonathan placed the call on the speakerphone, but muted the call so he could speak to Cassandra.

"Who is this, Cassandra?" Jonathan asked concerned.

"That's him, Sebastian Daniels, the man I met in San Diego" she said, nearly hysterical.

"Calm down Cassandra, you are safe, I am here with you," Jonathan assured her.

"Why won't he leave me alone?" she asked, shaking her head.

"Ask him what he wants?" Jonathan told her.

"I don't want to know, I want him out of my life!" she sobbed.

"If you are too afraid, I understand, but this creep is not done with you yet apparently," Jonathan told her plainly.

"I don't know what to say" she told Jonathan.

Jonathan quickly wrote down what she should say.

"I gave you the money you asked for so why are you still in Dallas and calling me?" she asked nervously.

"You messed up my plans by moving to Dallas and you made me kill someone close to me, but I found out the charges were dropped against you so now you owe me more money?" the caller told her.

"You can't blame that one me," Cassandra said, reading what Jonathan wrote.

"I had a good thing going and you ruined it, so I have to ruin you," the caller said.

"Please leave me alone, what will it take for you to leave me alone for good," Cassandra read her next line.

"The price has doubled, $10,000," the caller demanded.

"It will take time for me to get that much money," she said.

"You have one week," he demanded, ending the call.

Cassandra sobbed uncontrollably and Jonathan was unable to console her. Jonathan had his driver take a detour to the Ritz-Carlton hotel. He called ahead to let Taylor and Naomi know he was on his way with Cassandra, as well as Sergeant McLaughlin. Taylor did not like what he heard. It was too reminiscent of last year but this time it was Naomi's friend involved with a crazed man.

"Naomi, I do not like the way this investigation is headed. I think we should seriously consider letting the Dallas police handle it baby," Taylor implored.

"Taylor, Cassandra needs us right now, please reconsider," she said.

Taylor held Naomi close, deeply concerned. "Naomi, I need you safe. You can't let what happened in the past make you feel guilty," he told her.

"I know you are concerned, and I love you for it," she told him, gently touching his chest.

"The fear or thought of you being in danger triggers something in me. I would hurt anyone that tried to harm you and that's a side of me I never would want you to see again," Taylor shared.

"I promise to be careful and let the police handle anything dangerous. I just need to be able to assist Cassandra," she told him quietly, to calm the tension.

Taylor pulled her close to him, holding her as if she were a fragile doll.

The mere hint of harm coming to Naomi, his partner in life, the other half of his soul, sent a jolt of concern straight to his core. It was a sinister whisper, a shadow that crept along the edges of his consciousness, painting scenarios too harrowing to voice. His thoughts raced back to last year in Washington DC. But now he imagined faceless threats, each more terrifying than the last, all converging on the one person who meant everything to him.

His hands, usually so steady and sure, trembled ever so slightly with the weight of his unspoken worries. Taylor's heart raced, an unsure rhythm that seemed to keep time with his racing thoughts. "What if?" The question was a phantom that haunted him, a relentless ghost that echoed through the chambers of his heart.

Taylor felt a surge of anger at his own perceived powerlessness, a fiery impulse to do something, anything, to ensure Naomi's safety. Yet, it was tempered by the knowledge that he couldn't shield her from the risk of potential harm, couldn't be her guardian against every conceivable threat. It was a battle he fought within himself, a war between his instinct to protect Naomi and the reality of uncertainty.

As he turned away from the window, Taylor made a silent vow, he would not let fear rule him. He would be vigilant, yes, but he would also cherish every moment, every smile, every tender touch. For in the end, it was love, their shared bond, that was the greatest defense against the darkness of the world.

"You mean everything to me, I need you to know that" he whispered softly, summoning his peaceful side, gently kissing her lips.

"I do know, and I will not do anything without you knowing and I plan to work with a team so I will not be alone. Will you be on my team?" Naomi smiled, softening his mood.

"Yes I will," he said, totally committed to her in every way.

Jonathan and Cassandra arrived within minutes of Sergeant McLaughlin, who was dressed in street clothes, and driving his personal vehicle. When Cassandra saw Naomi, she collapsed in her arms defeated. Naomi held her friend to console her as Jonathan recounted what occurred in his car. Cassandra cried while hearing the conversation replayed. Jonathan had the wherewithal to record the conversation with his dictation recorder. Sergeant McLaughlin could not believe his ears, not only did the perpetrator confess to his previous crimes of extortion and murder, but he was also attempting to extort more money from Cassandra.

Cassandra felt helpless knowing this nightmare was not over but only getting worse. Her thoughts were racing, unable to focus on the conversation going on around her. All she heard were muffled voices. She was beyond distraught.

Then she broke her silence, "My family," she whimpered.

"Don't worry Cassandra, your family is safe. I sent uniformed officers to pick them up before I left the precinct," Sergeant McLaughlin reassured her.

"Can I see them?" she asked quietly, her voice almost childish.

"Of course, I will take you to them when we leave here," he told her.

Her family was officially in protective custody due to the serious nature of the investigation now.

"I am going to need your cell phone Cassandra in case he calls again," McLaughlin said.

She relinquished her phone as if it were contaminated, using two fingers to remove it from her purse.

"Sergeant McLaughlin, do you really think he is still in Dallas?" Naomi asked.

"I would say if he is bold enough to call Mrs. Collins, he is bold enough for anything. But I do know this, I plan to catch this bastard before he can hurt anyone else," McLaughlin promised.

"How can we help?" Naomi asked, eager to end her friend's suffering.

"You can help by trying to get an ID on this lunatic," he told Naomi.

"We have a week to identify him before his next move," Taylor said.

Taylor was all in after hearing the tape-recording and seeing firsthand the impact it had on Cassandra. He now understood why Naomi did not want to leave her friend. They definitely had their work cut out for them and did not want to waste a moment of time.

Sergeant McLaughlin drove Cassandra to her home so she could pack a few of her belongings. She quickly packed her bag and included a few personal items for her husband and son. She would not feel safe again until this man was behind bars. The drive to the safe house seemed like an eternity for her but she would soon be reunited with her family. Cassandra took a deep breath when she saw her husband, her hands shaking slightly as she clasped them together for strength.

"I know this is difficult to hear Charles and that's the last thing I ever wanted to bring to our family," she began, her voice steady but laced with a hint of fear, "but we are in danger and it's my fault."

Charles's face hardened as his protective instincts kicked in.

"We are not paying another dime," he said sternly. "Didn't you say you hired an investigator?"

"Yes, remember Naomi from New York. I contacted her office. She agreed to help me, help us," Cassandra told him.

"I thought the two of you were no longer friends," Charles wondered.

"It was a misunderstanding on my part," Cassandra said.

"I feel like a failure not being able to protect you and our son, Cassandra," Charles told her, hanging his head in disappointment.

He had always been their rock, the one who fixed the broken toys and chased away nightmares. But now, as the world outside descended into madness, his usual bravado felt like a frail mask. The news had been clear: no one was safe, and the danger was approaching fast. Charles' hands trembled as he turned momentarily, the thought of police protection was too much to bear.

"I'll keep you safe," he whispered, more to himself than to Cassandra. But the words felt hollow, a promise he wasn't sure he could keep. The thought of failing them, of being unable to shield them from the storm, clawed at his insides. He was supposed to be the protector, the defender. Yet, at that moment, he felt as vulnerable as a leaf in the wind, desperately wishing for the strength he feared he didn't possess.

"The world out there is falling apart, and I... What if I can't keep you safe?" He second guessed himself, self-doubt creeping in.

"You're doing everything you can. That's all we can ask for. We don't expect you to be a superhero, just the man we love," Cassandra assured him, exhibiting a show of strength that had been stolen from her.

"But what if that's not enough?" Charles' voice cracked, his eyes glistening with unshed tears. "What if my love can't stop what's coming?"

"It's not about stopping it, Charles," Cassandra replied, her voice firm yet gentle. "It's about facing it together. As long as we have each other, we can get through anything."

Charles looked up at her, the fear in his eyes slowly giving way to determination.

"Together," he echoed, a promise forged in the quiet strength of their shared determination. He felt a resurgence of his power. He summoned the courage and strength his family needed from him at that very moment. Charles had a new resolve to do whatever he needed to make sure his wife and son was safe from all dangers.

Naomi called the agency to update Margaret Regis on their progress and the direction the case had taken. She would enlist the entire agency on this case to identify the culprit as quickly as possible. Since Cassandra was safe in police protection, Naomi was comfortable returning to New Orleans to utilize all of their resources. Margaret arranged for the Sylvesters to return to New Orleans via private jet. Naomi quickly packed their luggage while Taylor contacted the front desk for an early check out.

Naomi and Taylor's flight touched down at Louis Armstrong Airport just as dawn was breaking. They quickly collected their luggage and made their way off the plane to the car service area, where Naomi noticed someone holding up a sign that read 'Secure Justice.' She nudged Taylor, pointing out the sign and they immediately walked toward the driver.

"Are you Mr. Sylvester?" the driver questioned.

"Yes sir," Taylor confirmed.

The driver escorted them to the awaiting black sedan parked in a reserved location. Taylor opened the car door for Naomi and followed her inside. The driver started the engine and quickly navigated through the light airport traffic, then merged onto the I-10 East towards the Central Business District (CBD). The early morning light cast long shadows across the highway, and the city's iconic skyline began to emerge in the distance like a mirage welcoming them home. The air was thick with humidity, a tangible reminder that they were indeed home. Taylor rolled down the back windows, letting the warm breeze carry in the sounds of the waking city. The faint hum of traffic blended with the occasional sound of a distant trumpet, and the scent of coffee wafted in from a nearby café.

As they approached the CBD, the sun crested the horizon, spilling golden light between the buildings. The city's pulse quickened; streetcars rumbled to life, and early risers filled the sidewalks. Taylor's eyes were drawn to the reflection of the sun on the glass facades, a stark contrast to the dark case they came back to work on.

Naomi took a sip from her travel mug, the bitter coffee a sharp contrast to the sweet beignets she planned to grab before heading to the office. She wanted to bring a treat with them to the office because she wanted her staff's attention as soon as they arrived at the agency, but first they stopped home to shower and change clothes.

"Shower for two to save time?" Taylor suggested.

"Only if it includes a neck massage," Naomi smiled.

"Oh, it definitely does," Taylor promised.

"You're too good to me Mr. Sylvester and you have the best hands," she said as all the tension rolled down the drain with the warm soapy water.

To Naomi's surprise, Margaret had already given out assignments to the staff as well as the freelance investigators they used. Margaret worked with the team who was conducting a deep dive into Sebastian Daniels. They poured through every facet of his life to find some connection to Cassandra Collins or her old job. Sheila worked with the team who was responsible for locating the registrants at the convention Cassandra attended in San Diego. This was the most daunting and tedious task, so more resources and manpower were required.

Taylor contacted his two friends Anthony and Joseph to help as well. It was literally all hands-on deck. He enlisted Joseph to work with the freelance investigators since his background was in surveillance and he was able to find people that did not leave a digital footprint. Anthony would be on standby to him if he felt Naomi was in real danger. Taylor worked on the financial component to see who might have accessed Cassandra's bank accounts. Cassandra's life was being examined with a fine-tooth comb, a necessary violation to discover her tormentor.

Naomi assigned her freelance investigators to dissect the voice recording to see if they could get a lead. They also combed through the hotel surveillance footage to find any sightings of the suspect or anyone suspicious. They divided the video footage up frame by frame to examine each image captured for any possible clue. Joseph showed them new techniques to review the footage.

Naomi reached out to Sergeant McLaughlin to contact the San Diego Police Department to see if they had any reports of women being dosed with Rohypnol or its street name 'Roofie.' Cassandra may not have been his only victim. Naomi could not help but wonder if she hadn't been caught up with her previous case this might not have happened. She became angry all over again with Henry Williams and his twisted fantasy of being with her. Here was another man attempting to shatter the dreams of an innocent woman. Naomi put her focus back on Cassandra since they had less than a week to work with. Every minute mattered, but she knew her staff needed a break because everyone had worked through lunch, and it was now after 5:00 PM.

Naomi ordered dinner for the entire staff and once dinner arrived, they all took a break to eat, only a few stayed at the office after dinner. By 6:30 PM, with no new leads, Naomi sent those who were left home to start fresh the next morning. Taylor entered her office, briefcase in hand motioning towards the door.

"You need to get some rest baby, and we have to go pick up Saint," Taylor said in a gentle concerned voice.

Naomi knew he was right, so she did not put up any resistance. She collected the papers she was working on, turned off her desk lamp and picked up her purse. Taylor drove instead of calling for a car service. He wanted to be alone with his wife. The car ride was quiet, soft music played on the radio as Naomi rested her head on the back of the car seat. No words were spoken, Taylor simply held her hand the entire ride. They stopped at the puppy breeder to pick up their fur baby. Just seeing his sweet face lifted Naomi's spirits. She cradled his tiny body as he slept all the way home.

Taylor and Naomi found themselves in the quiet comfort of their living room. The day's demands had been unrelenting, but now, in each other's presence, the stress began to melt away. Naomi placed Saint in his puppy bed, then nestled into the crook of Taylor's arm, her head resting against his broad chest, where she could hear the steady beat of his heart. A soft sigh escaped her lips as Taylor's fingers gently traced patterns along her arm, his touch light but filled with affection. Naomi melted under his caress.

"I know you had a rough day" Taylor's voice was a soothing baritone, a sound that always seemed to ease her worries.

"You could say that again," Naomi replied, her eyes closed as she savored the warmth of his body against hers. "But right now, I can't think of a better place to be."

Taylor grunted, the sound vibrating through his chest. "I've been looking forward to this moment all day," he confessed, pressing a tender kiss to the top of her head.

The room was filled with soft notes of jazz playing in the background, the melody slow and intimate. It was their song, the one that had danced around them on their wedding day, and now it was wrapped around them like a familiar embrace. With a gentle pull, Taylor encouraged Naomi to look up at him. Their eyes met, and for a moment, the world outside ceased to exist. There was only the two of them, their sleeping puppy, the music, and the love that had only grown stronger with each passing day.

"Let's forget about work and everything else for tonight," Taylor whispered, his thumb caressing her cheek.

Naomi nodded, her heart swelling with emotion. "Just you and me," she agreed, her voice barely above a whisper. Taylor leaned down, kissing her gently on her lips reminding her of every reason she loved him. And as they lost themselves in each other's gaze, the rest of the evening promised nothing but tenderness, passion, and the quiet joy of being together.

Chapter 7

The first light of dawn filtered through the sheer curtains, casting a warm glow across their bedroom. Taylor and Naomi, entwined in the soft embrace of sleep, lay peaceful amidst the tangled sheets. The night had been long, a storm of emotions and whispered admissions of love and promises, leaving them free in the sea of openness that only the dark hours can bring. As the sun rose higher, its rays caressed Naomi's face, luring her from the depths of dreams. Her eyelids fluttered open, revealing the color of the bright sky that now watched over them. She turned to find Taylor, still lost in sleep, his chest rising and falling in the steady rhythm that spoke of deep rest. A smile, tender and full of love, graced her lips as she watched him, her protector and confidant.

The room around them was silent, except for the distant chorus of the waking world outside their window. It was a new day, fresh with new possibilities. Naomi reached out, her fingers brushing against Taylor's arm, feeling the warmth of his skin. He stirred, a soft groan escaping him as he too began to cross the bridge back to consciousness. Their eyes met, and in that moment, they found the unspoken words of the night before, the fears shared, and the comfort given. They didn't need to speak; the silence between them was filled with understanding and a shared resolve to face whatever the day might bring, together.

With a gentle nudge, they rose, the bed surrendering its hold on them. The air was cool, a stark contrast to the warmth of their bed, but it was invigorating, a reminder that life was waiting for them beyond these four walls. Taylor showered as Naomi squeezed in the last few minutes of rest the bed was offering. Taylor dressed quickly, heading to the kitchen to prepare breakfast and feed Saint. After her shower Naomi met him in the kitchen greeted by the welcoming smell of chicory coffee. She held the hot coffee cup firmly as she sipped the strong brew. Taylor pulled Naomi close to him as she drank her coffee.

"Did you rest well?" Taylor asked, squeezing her a little tighter by her waist.

"Definitely Mr. Sylvester. Thank you for taking care of me," Naomi smiled, touching his arm.

"I have a good feeling we will get a break in the case," Taylor said.

"I surely hope so baby," she told him.

"Saint has his extra bed and belongings packed and ready to go," Taylor smiled.

"We're bringing him to the office?" Naomi questioned, with a bit of excitement.

"His breed is not good to leave alone so young, plus he needs to get to know us and our habits," Taylor explained.

"Ok Mr. Puppy Whisperer," she joked.

The drive to the agency was quiet, a little small talk about their new puppy. When they arrived, the conference room was filled with fresh pastries, coffee, and orange juice. The agency had been abuzz since 6:00 AM. Naomi and Taylor entered the office with their new family addition, Saint. Margaret and her team were hard at work, tirelessly trying to uncover clues to solve this puzzle with the limited pieces available. The initiative Margaret took extremely impressed Naomi.

Margaret entered Naomi's office with a satisfied expression, but the ball of black fur Naomi held distracted her momentarily.

"Naomi, I think we may have found something," Margaret announced.

"What it is?" Naomi asked, praying for a much-needed break.

"We found a Sebastain Daniels living in San Diego, but it also looks like he has lived several places," Margaret told her.

On paper Sebastian Daniels was a single man who had no family and recently moved to the San Diego area according to his social media. Margaret's team poured through Sebastian's social media account, but the account seemed to be a dummy account. There were no personal pictures, no digital signature.

"What can you piece together?" Naomi asked, her attention was redirected to these new findings.

"We think 'Sebastian Daniels' is just an alias but for who is the missing component," she said.

"Margaret, I could kiss you!" Naomi said with a glimmer of hope for their first real lead in the case.

The surveillance team had a lead as well. They found footage of 'Sebastian Daniels' speaking with a man whose back was to the camera and the man appeared to be following him to the elevator. Naomi was so excited to have two new pieces of the puzzle, but it still did not make any sense. She shifted her little fur ball to her other arm causing Saint to whimper.

"Now who is this beautiful baby?" Margaret asked.

"This is Saint. Taylor surprised me with him when we came back from Fiji," she smiled.

"He's gorgeous Naomi," Margaret said, scooping him up from Naomi's arms.

Saint let out a tiny yarn, stretching his little body as Margaret held him.

"Do you mind him being in the office?" Naomi asked.

"He's a part of the family now and look at those unique eyes," Margaret smiled as she headed out the door Saint in tow to formally introduce him to everyone.

Naomi contacted Sergeant McLaughlin to fill him in on what they discovered.

"Good morning, Sergeant," her eyes perked as she spoke, "we have two new leads to share. Did your department question any hotel staff?" Naomi asked.

"We only questioned the witness that saw Cassandra, unfortunately," he confessed.

"My surveillance team found footage of the victim with another man that may possibly be his killer or the last person to see him alive. In the video looks like Sebastian knew the man. Sergeant, if you could review more footage, we may be able to see which way they went in the hotel. I also think Sebastian may have a bigger role in this," Naomi told him.

"Mrs. Sylvester you have wonderful insight and a great agency working for you," Sergeant McLaughlin commented. "I will request a copy of the autopsy from the coroner immediately, as well as send an officer back to the hotel to interview staff on duty the night of the murder," he told Naomi.

"How is Cassandra and her family doing?" Naomi questioned.

"Mrs. Collins is a bit on edge but that is normal. Her husband has been supportive which is helpful in this situation," he told her.

Naomi was relieved to hear that Cassandra was safe and that her family was making the most of an inconvenient situation.

"We also found a potential lead in San Diego, where 'Sebastain Daniels' lived and the initial contact with the suspect occurred. I would like to speak with hotel staff at the Marriott Marquis, San Diego Marina. Do you have any contacts in the police department in San Diego I could speak with?" Naomi asked.

A point of contact would be ideal, and Sergeant McLaughlin had one for Naomi. His former weapons trainer Carl Augustine, transferred to the San Diego police department three years ago.

"What do you need from them?" he asked Naomi

"I would like to see any cases reported of women being given roofies at hotels or night clubs, no matter how insignificant. I also would like authorization to speak with staff at the Marriott Hotel," she told him.

"Do you plan to go to San Diego?" He asked her.

"I think it may be a good idea," she said.

"Carl should be able to assist," Sergeant McLaughlin assured her.

"Ok I will make travel arrangements as soon as possible," Naomi said as Taylor walked in her office.

"Travel arrangements to where?" He questioned, eyes wide.

"Is that Mr. Sylvester?" Sergeant McLaughlin asked.

"Yes, that's Taylor, I will fill him in after the call."

Naomi was afraid Taylor would not agree with her going to San Diego but to Naomi's surprise he made the arrangements himself.

"I booked you two tickets to San Diego. It's your choice who to take with you because I am not sending you solo. You can take Anthony with you or your overprotective handsome husband," Taylor said.

Naomi smiled, "That good feeling you had this morning about getting a lead rang true and hands down, you are always my choice."

"This would be our inaugural trip to San Diego, sorry it's not under different circumstances," he noted.

"We need a puppy sitter now unless you want Saint with us," Naomi realized.

Margaret popped her head in the office door, "No need to ask, he can stay with me while you are away, and I'll bring him to work every day to get him accustomed to his new surroundings."

"Thank you, Margaret we appreciate everything you do," Naomi smiled.

"I don't mind it at all, he'll bring a little excitement to my life," she laughed.

"You are a life saver Margaret," Taylor smiled.

As the plane descended, the city of San Diego unfolded below like a vibrant tapestry. Naomi could see the Pacific Ocean shimmering in the distance.

Naomi squeezed Taylor's hand, her eyes wide with anticipation. "Look at that view," she whispered, as the aircraft's wheels touched down with a gentle thud. Exiting the plane and retrieving their luggage was an unexpectedly quick process. When they stepped out of the airport, a salty sea breeze hit their noses. The city welcomed them with open arms. Palm trees swayed as if to the rhythm of their excitement, and the distant sound of waves promised adventures yet to come. They hailed a taxi, and the driver greeted them with a laid-back smile.

Their taxi merged through the bustling streets of the city, Naomi's eyes pivoted from one sight to another. The historic Gaslamp Quarter, the majestic Coronado Bridge, and the lavish Balboa Park bypassed their windows, each landmark a promise of memories to be made and soon, the impressive façade of the Marriott Marquis came into view. Its immense glass structure reflected the last rays of the mid-morning sun, making it look like a beacon of luxury and relaxation.

"Wow," Naomi breathed out, her eyes wide with wonder. "It's even more beautiful than the pictures," Taylor held Naomi's hand in response, equally in awe.

Once they arrived at the hotel, Taylor checked in, and a bellhop led them to their room on the 15th floor. The bellhop opened the door to reveal a spacious, elegantly furnished room with floor-to-ceiling windows that offered a panoramic view of the marina.

Naomi and Taylor stood by the window, watching as the boats dipped gently in the water and the city lights began to twinkle to life. Taylor wrapped his arms around Naomi from behind, and she leaned back into his embrace. They stood quietly taking in the wonderful views. New Orleans was a city with waterways, but this was different. Taylor admired several of the yachts off in the distance. He pictured the two of them sailing away for a weekend excursion when this case was over.

"I wish we were here under different circumstances," Taylor shared.

"Any time spent with you is perfect but once this is all over can we come back?" she murmured.

"Most definitely baby, you read my mind," he said.

The Marriott Marquis, with its promise of new experiences and the comfort of each other's company, was the perfect backdrop for their stay in San Diego.

As Taylor and Naomi entered the glass doors, the fluorescent lights of the San Diego Police Station cast a sterile glow over the room. Naomi looked around the police station, observing her new surroundings. Desks were cluttered with case files, coffee cups, and the occasional personal photo. The persistent clack of keyboards was interrupted by the rustle of radio dispatch. Naomi informed one of the officers that they had a meeting with Lieutenant Augustine. He acknowledged that they did and escorted them to his office.

Lieutenant Carl Augustine stood from his chair, eyes narrowed as he scrutinized Naomi and Taylor before he spoke. Sergeant McLaughlin only asked if he would be willing to meet with them on short notice.

Lieutenant Carl Augustine had the kind of presence that filled a room—a tall, broad-shouldered figure with a salt-and-pepper beard that perfectly framed his strong jawline, his presence commanding yet reassuring. His skin was a smooth, dark hue that contrasted sharply against the crisp white of his shirt and the gleaming badge that adorned his chest. His uniform, was immaculate, seeming to mirror his work ethic: disciplined, unwavering, and respected by all.

The creases in his trousers were sharp enough to cut paper, and his shoes had a luster that spoke of meticulous care. Despite the years etched into the lines of his face, there was a youthfulness in his eyes, a spark that told of a man who loved his work and carried his responsibilities with pride. His eyes, a piercing shade of brown, scanned the room with an intensity that contradicted his calm demeanor. Carl was not just any lieutenant; he was a man who had climbed the ranks with grit and grace, earning the respect of his peers and the community he served. Standing at an imposing six-foot-two, his physique was the result of years of disciplined training, yet there was a gentleness to him that softened his otherwise stern appearance.

Lieutenant Augustine's demeanor was calm and collected, a stillness that contradicted the keen alertness behind his observant eyes. He exuded quiet confidence, the kind that inspired trust and respect from his peers and the community he served. Lieutenant Augustine was more than just a figure of authority; he was a pillar in the tapestry of the city, a guardian of the peace he had sworn to uphold. He moved with purpose, each step measured and assured, the result of navigating both the literal and figurative streets of law enforcement. Raised in the vibrant neighborhoods of Dallas, he carried with him the lessons of community and kinship, values that now infused his leadership style with empathy and a deep sense of justice. Augustine's journey from Dallas to San Diego had been marked by a trail of commendations and breakthrough cases. He was the kind of officer who remembered names and faces, who listened more than he spoke, and when he did, his voice carried the weight of experience and the softness of empathy. His move to San Diego years ago had been a promotion well-earned, and he had since become a cornerstone of the community, bridging gaps, and building trust where it was needed most.

"So, Mrs. Sylvester, what brings you to my precinct?" He asked with a mix of skepticism and respect.

Naomi placed a leather briefcase on the desk, popping it open to reveal an organized chaos of files and photos.

"A case, Lieutenant. One that I believe you may be extremely interested in," Naomi said with a hint of urgency.

Lieutenant Augustine raised an eyebrow, his interest piqued despite his reservations. He motioned for Naomi to continue as he took a sip from his steaming coffee.

"We've been tracking a murder suspect, who we have not been able to identify yet, and he also preys on women by drugging them, then later attempting to blackmail them. We think there may be more victims," Naomi leaned forward as she spoke.

Lieutenant Augustine's eyes glanced at the briefcase, taking in the evidence Naomi had laid out.

"And are you proposing Mrs. Sylvester?" Augustine asked, intrigued.

"A collaboration. We share our resources and my information. Together, we can catch this extortionist and murderer before he strikes again," Naomi said with a slight smile.

Lieutenant Augustine considered her proposition, the gears turning in his head. He knew the rules, the lines that should not to be crossed, but he also knew the frustration of cold cases and the allure of a fresh lead.

"Alright, Mrs. Sylvester. Let's see what you've got," Lieutenant Augustine said, extending his hand.

Naomi and Lieutenant Augustine shook hands, as if an unspoken agreement were hanging between them. Naomi laid out all the details she had of the case and asked if he was willing to share any cases that may have involved extortion or date rape drugging. Augustine called for his secretary and asked her to pull out any unsolved cases that were similar to Cassandra's story. Naomi also shared the lead that Sergeant McLaughlin was following back in Dallas.

"So how does a private investigator from New Orleans end up in San Diego?" Augustine asked her.

"Well sir, I am just following wherever the clues take me," Naomi explained.

"And is this your partner?" he asked, motioning to Taylor.

"Yes, in all aspects," Naomi proudly smiled.

"My name is Taylor Sylvester, Naomi's husband and business partner," Taylor said haughtily, extending his hand.

"How long have you been working together?" Augustine asked.

"Naomi and I have worked together in various capacities," Taylor explained.

"I was a DEA agent for years and decided my talent could be used in other ways. Taylor and I have known each other since college and his legal expertise has come in handy. I finally succumbed to his charming personality and married him," Naomi beamed.

"You're a fascinating woman," Augustine concluded. "And I wouldn't place you as an investigator Mr. Sylvester," he added.

"I am a corporate attorney, primarily but this young lady is training me to be her top investigator for legal cases. We are partners in Secure Justice Agency as well, but I still have my law firm," Taylor shared.

"And how did you really end up here?" Augustine pressed her.

"The client is a friend of mine who was the victim of a deadly catfishing type scheme. She let her guard down for a moment, one that has resulted in shattered dreams. That moment cost her an excellent job, her career, her home, and almost her family," Naomi told him, emphasizing the seriousness of this investigation.

Before Naomi could continue, Carl Augustine's secretary returned with folders in her hand.

"I was able to find these for you sir," she said presenting him with the folders.

Lieutenant Augustine looked through the folders briefly. There were two unsolved cases of women who reported being drugged and violated at a convention. Neither had any memory of what happened to warrant an investigation. This was another big piece to their puzzle, and it also appeared they uncovered a serial predator.

"Would I be able to speak with these women?" Naomi wondered, hoping the answer would be yes.

Lieutenant Augustine thought silently as he reviewed each file more thoroughly. He looked up at Naomi before he responded.

"I feel like department failed these women," he said softly handing her the files.

"Is that yes?" she asked cautiously.

"You can speak with them in the presence of one my officers," He agreed.

Lieutenant Augustine asked his secretary to contact the two victims to schedule an interview as soon as possible. Naomi was one step closer to solving Cassandra's case and making sure a murderer would be apprehended. She wondered how many other victims were out there. The very thought sickened her that someone could be so evil.

Amazingly interviews were scheduled for both victims later that afternoon so Naomi and Taylor would return to the police department. Lieutenant Augustine recommended a lunch spot for the couple, while he continued to review the case files. Lunch was quiet and uneventful, Naomi barely ate any of her food.

"I know you have a lot on your mind," Taylor said, concerned.

"I just have a feeling we are missing something," Naomi muttered.

"Well, you need energy to think clear and if you don't eat, I'm afraid that won't be helpful," he cautioned.

"You're right of course," she surrendered.

"What about dessert? I saw a brownie on the dessert menu, want to share it?" Taylor offered, nudging her leg under the table.

"Ok, why not," she managed a smile.

Taylor waved for their waitress, ordering the brownie and two scoops of vanilla ice cream. A few minutes later, the waitress returned with a chocolate wonder surrounded by two heaps of ice cream drizzled with caramel and fudge.

Taylor smiled as the sweet treat caused Naomi's face to light up. A playful game ensued as they took turns feeding each other the delicious delight.

Chapter 8

Lieutenant Augustine contacted Naomi to return to the police department since their first appointment was enroute. The first case's victim was that of a wealthy businesswoman, who was the CEO of a computer tech company. Her wardrobe reflected her impeccable taste and wealth. Her attire was an exquisite distraction from the hidden truth. She entered the investigation room cautiously. Naomi and Lieutenant Augustine sat across a shiny black table from Ms. Tanya Wilson. The room was glaring, illuminated by the harsh glow of a single overhead light.

Lieutenant Augustine began the interview, flipping open a notepad "Ms. Wilson, can you tell me what happened on the night of March 15th?"

"I was at the annual tech convention at the Ritz in Laguna Niguel. The final night was our main event, a formal gala. After the gala, I... I don't remember much. It's all a blur," Tanya Wilson recalled, clutching her designer purse, her voice strained.

"Do you recall accepting any drinks from someone at the event?" Lieutenant Augustine asked.

"Yes, a gentleman from the convention offered me a glass of champagne. He said it was a special vintage. I thought nothing of it at the time," Tanya Wilson said.

"Try to describe this gentleman. Anything you remember could be crucial," Naomi broke her silence, leaning in, her tone gentle but exploring.

"He was pleasant, well-dressed in a tuxedo with paisley jacket. A silver ring with some sort of crest was on his right index finger... that's all I can recall," she said, closing her eyes tightly as if forcing the buried memory to the surface.

"We'll look into it. Now, after you drank the champagne, what's the next thing you remember?" Lieutenant Augustine took over, scribbling notes.

"Waking up in my hotel suite, feeling... violated. My head was throbbing, and there was a note on my bedside table," Ms. Wilson said with hurt in her eyes.

"A note? What did it say?" Naomi could not help chiming in.

"It said, 'I'll be in touch, Tanya,'" her composed state cracked, allowing the tears she once contained to betray her.

Naomi looked at Lieutenant Augustine and he nodded, authorizing her to continue questioning Ms. Wison.

"Have you had any further communication with him?" Naomi continued with her questions.

"I received an envelope at my office a few days later with lewd pictures and a demand of $5000 or the pictures would be shared," Ms. Wilson said shaking her head, softly sobbing.

Namoi gently took her hand, "We'll do everything we can to find who did this. You're safe now, Ms. Wilson."

"Why didn't you report it to the police the next morning? Lieutenant Augustine asked.

"I hate the fact that I gave in and paid the money," she conceded.

Tanya recalled sitting in her office as her hands trembled preparing the envelope. The stress of defeat weighed heavily on her chest, an invisible force that seemed to constrict her every breath. She had fought against the surge of intimidation, but the relentless waves of guilt had finally eroded her resolve. With each crisp hundred-dollar bill that she placed inside, a piece of her dignity seemed to tear away, she was being violated again.

She sat alone in her office in silence that was disturbed only by the rustle of currency and the distant hum of the city. It was in this stillness that Tanya's thoughts screamed the loudest, a conflict of fear, despair, and anger. She knew that this act of submission was a surrender not just to the faceless perpetrator that demanded her submission but to her own dignity.

As she sealed the envelope, her fingers remained on the flap as she contemplated her decision. There was no turning back now. This was the cost of safety, of peace, a price paid not in money, but in shards of her soul. She contacted **Speedy Courier Service** as instructed, the envelope was addressed with only the P.O. Box number provided. Tanya left the envelope in its designated spot, and as she walked away, she couldn't help but wonder if the true extortion was not of her wealth, but of her will to stand up for herself.

"I only reported the extortion because I realized they might try to ask for more and I could not trust the pictures would be destroyed. I hate myself for being so gullible," Tanya said.

"You are not to blame," Naomi told her as Tanya left the room.

Their next appointment was quite the opposite, Mrs. Cynthia Josephine, a middle-aged woman with a sturdy gaze that projected her calm demeanor. She was in her mid-fifties, but she was the epitome of timeless grace, with a presence that contradicted her middle age. Her skin, a rich and flawless mahogany, seemed to defy the very concept of time. Her eyes were dark and radiant and were framed by thick lashes that fluttered like the dainty wings of a butterfly, casting shadows on her high cheekbones. Her ebony curls fell around her shoulders in a natural halo and as she walked, her head movement revealed hidden strands of silver—an indication of her wisdom and experience.

Mrs. Josephine could easily pass for early thirties. Naomi was captured by her poise and beauty which made the questioning that was about to take place more difficult. The air was thick with tension, the kind that comes before a storm. Lieutenant Augustine introduced himself and Naomi and informed Mrs. Josephine that they read over her case file. She had provided as many details as possible but was only reporting about the attempt at extortion.

"Mrs. Josephine do you have any idea who put something in your drink?" Naomi began.

"I don't know his name, but he was definitely at the convention I attended last month," she told Naomi.

"What type of convention did you attend?" Naomi asked.

"My husband and I are realtors, and this was our annual real estate convention recognizing top sellers," She explained.

"Mrs. Josephine, we think your case is related to several others," Naomi shared.

"I understand this is difficult, Mrs. Josephine, but we need to know everything," Lieutenant Augustine added, his voice firm yet empathetic. "The extortion notes, the threats—why haven't you paid them?" Naomi asked.

Cynthia's lips pressed into a thin line, her hands folded neatly on her lap.

"Because I refuse to be bullied by cowards hiding behind anonymous letters," she replied, her voice unwavering. "My husband and I worked hard for our money, and I won't have it siphoned away by criminals," she said sternly.

Naomi nodded, scribbling notes in her pad. "Do you have any idea who might be behind this?"

A flicker of something passed over Cynthia's face—fear, perhaps, or anger. "No," she said, a little too quickly. "But I've lived long enough to know that succumbing to blackmail only opens the door to more demands."

The Lieutenant leaned forward, his eyes searching Cynthia's. "We can offer protection, Mrs. Josephine. Witness programs, surveillance, or patrol officers," he assured.

Cynthia raised her hand, stopping him at mid-sentence. "I appreciate it, Lieutenant, but I won't hide. I won't be intimidated. I've faced worse than this," she informed him.

"I appreciate your stance Mrs. Josephine, but in your statement, you said the attacker's drug wore off, which was how you got away from him. Can you explain?" Naomi probed further.

"I remember being at the bar area to get drinks for me and another realtor, next thing I remember is yelling for this man to get out of my hotel room, which I don't even know how I got to the room," she told Naomi.

"Mrs. Josephine do you take any medication?" Naomi asked.

"That's a strange question to ask me young lady," she said, half offended but still intrigued.

"Humor me if you don't mind," Naomi told her, looking toward Lieutenant Augustine, who also looked lost to her line of questioning.

"I take a blood pressure medication, Lisinopril and two for migraines, Cafergot and Fiorinal," Mrs. Josephine shared.

"Ah, makes sense," Naomi said shaking her head.

"Only to you it makes sense," Mrs. Josephine chuckled nervously.

"So sorry, my background is pharmacy so that's what I was eluding to. The drug we believe was used to spike your drink was counteracted so to speak by your migraine medication, both of which contain caffeine, which was truly fortunate for you," Naomi explained.

"Nice work Naomi," Lieutenant Augustine smiled.

Lieutenant Augustine's respect for Naomi grew. The knowledge and professionalism she showed during both interviews impressed him. All reservations he had about working with her disappeared.

"Just a few more questions if you don't mind Mrs. Josephine. Did you get a clear look at his face or notice any distinguishing marks that may have stood out? How was the extortion request delivered to you?" Naomi probed further.

Mrs. Josephine took her time thinking about the questions before responding.

"I remember he had dark hair and eyes, olive brown complexion and he had a large ring that he nervously twisted on his finger. And the envelope was delivered to our office by courier two days later," she relayed.

"You have been a tremendous help," Lieutenant Augustine said. He stood up, extending his hand for her to shake.

"We'll do everything we can to catch whoever is responsible. You're not alone in this," he reassured her.

As Cynthia shook his hand, the Lieutenant saw the resolve in her eyes. This was a woman who wouldn't bend, wouldn't break. As refined as Cynthia Josephine appeared, her demeanor told a different story, that she could easily take on any man and win in a fight. Naomi and Lieutenant Augustine were determined to stand with her, no matter what happened. They were a little closer to catching whoever was behind these assaults, armed with a few more pieces to the puzzle.

In Dallas the sun had just descended below the horizon, casting an eerie glow through the sheer curtains of the living room of their temporary living quarters. Nestled on the quiet outskirts of the city, the safe house stood as an unassertive beacon of security. From the outside, it appeared to be a derelict cottage, overgrown with ivy and with a renovation sign posted on the on the front door. The exterior was a carefully coordinated deception; behind the weathered exterior lay a state-of-the-art fortress.

The interior was a total contrast to the outside. The walls were reinforced with steel, and the windows were bulletproof, capable of withstanding high-caliber impacts. Surveillance cameras were in the corners of each room, outfitted with motion detection, their lenses barely visible, mixing seamlessly with the color scheme of the walls.

Each room was lightly furnished, concentrating on function over comfort, lacking any character. In the living area, a large monitor displayed feeds from the cameras, while another monitor showed a live map tracking the movements of anyone approaching the surrounding area.

The safe house was self-supporting, equipped with its own power source, a secure internet connection, and an underground water tank. The kitchen cabinets were stocked with non-perishable food, enough to last for months. A plain-clothed officer purchased any perishable items as needed.

In the center of the room, the family sat huddled together on the couch, their eyes reflecting the flicker of the news on the television. Charles kept his arm firmly around his wife, Cassandra, whose eyes were consumed with fear. Beside them, the son Brian sat, clutching his favorite stuffed animal, a sense of innocence lost too soon.

At each window and door, a police officer stood, their presence a constant reminder of the potential danger looming outside. The officers were stoic, their eyes scanning for any sign of the threat that had sent the Collins family into this state of high alert.

"Mommy, can I go outside and play?" Brian's voice was small, splitting the thick tension in the room.

"Soon, honey," Cassandra replied, her voice steady despite the fear she felt. "The police are here to make sure we're safe. We just have to stay inside for a little while longer, but you can play with your stuffed animal."

Charles squeezed her hand, a silent show of support. They both knew the gravity of the situation. She and her family would not be safe until the perpetrator was caught. The deadline to have the extortion money was two days away and Naomi and the Dallas police department were not close to catching him.

A knock at the door made everyone flinch. One of the officers moved to answer it, returning with a takeout order and drinks. Little Brian was excited, he got to eat out every day. As they ate in silence, the family found comfort in the small act of normalcy. It was a fleeting break from the weight of their current circumstances, a temporary lapse into the life they once knew. The phone rang, which startled them once more. It was Naomi with an update on the investigation.

"Hi Cassandra, we had a small break in the case. Two more victims came forward that we think were drugged by the same man that drugged you. We believe he is back in San Diego, and this is his sick playground," Naomi shared.

"Do you think he will come back here for the money?" Cassandra asked, worried.

"I honestly don't know what is driving him to answer that, but you are safe there with the police protecting you," Naomi assured her.

Naomi struggled with what she should share with Cassandra, not wanting to worry her any further but also, she did not want to betray the trust of the other victims who confided in her. These women desperately required her assistance and right now Naomi's hands were tied. She didn't know whether to stay in San Diego, travel to Dallas or return home. Naomi seriously needed a break in the case to end this nightmare for the women and her friend.

Chapter 9

Taylor met up with Naomi for an early dinner. She was quiet throughout the entire dinner, almost despondent. This case affected her more than she realized. She refused to be outwitted by the likes of this predator. Taylor could tell dinner was not on Naomi's mind. The drive back to the hotel was as quiet as dinner. They returned to the hotel to unwind. The room was drenched with the soft glow of the evening sun, casting elongated shadows across the floor. Naomi sat by the window, her eyes distant, lost in thought. What would her next step be?

Taylor watched her from the doorway, his heart aching at the sight of her so despondent. He crossed the room quietly and knelt beside her, taking her hand in his.

"Naomi," he whispered, his voice barely above the buzz of the breeze through the open window.

She turned to him, her eyes defeated.

"I am out of ideas, Taylor? How can I help these women?"

He squeezed her hand gently, a reassuring anchor in the storm of doubt.

"Together," he said firmly. "We move forward together. We face each hurdle as a team, and no matter what comes, we'll be side by side," he promised.

Naomi leaned into him, her head resting on his shoulder.

"I'm worried," she admitted, her voice muffled against his shirt.

"I know," Taylor replied, wrapping his arms around her. "But I also know that we're stronger than our fears. We've weathered storms before, and we'll do it again. And each time, we've come out a little stronger, a little closer. You're not alone in this, baby. Never alone," he told her.

The moonlight dripped through the sheer curtains, casting a peaceful glow across the room. The clock on the bedside table ticked softly, marking the passage of the late hours. In the dim light, Naomi's silhouette was a restless outline on the bed, her sleep disturbed by dreams that moved just out of reach of her consciousness. Taylor, lying beside her, stirred as he felt the tension in her body. He turned to face her, his eyes adjusting to the darkness. The crease between her eyebrows, the slight frown on her lips, were enough to tell him she was restless. He reached out, his hand finding hers under the cool sheets.

"Baby," he whispered, his voice a soothing comfort in the quiet of the night. "It's okay, I'm here."

Naomi's eyes flickered open, meeting Taylor's peaceful gaze. There was a vulnerability there, a silent appeal for comfort that she didn't need to voice. He knew. He always did. With a gentle tug, he pulled her closer, wrapping his arms around her. She moaned as she tried to readjust her body. She snuggled into his chest, her breaths slowly evening out as she listened to the steady beat of his heart. It was a familiar rhythm, a reminder of the numerous nights they had shared, of the bond that held them together through every storm.

"Shh," Taylor whispered, his lips pressing a soft kiss to her forehead.

"Let me be your anchor. Let your worries drift away. I've got you," he told her.

And in the sanctuary of his embrace, the restless whispers of the night faded. Naomi's body relaxed, her mind quietened by the presence of the man who stood by her through every high and low. Together, they drifted back into a tranquil sleep, the kind that only comes when two souls are intertwined in love and trust.

The first glow of daylight crept through the sheer curtains, casting a warm glow across the room. In the tranquility of the morning, the soft, rhythmic breathing of the couple filled the air, a testament to the deep slumber they had been in. As the sun rose higher, its rays gently embraced the face of Naomi, who stirred slightly, her eyelids fluttering open. The dreams of the night lingered in her mind, a sweet echo of the peace she felt. Beside her, Taylor lay still, the rise and fall of his chest the only movement. Naomi turned her head, her gaze settling on Taylor's serene expression. A smile graced her lips as she watched him, the quiet joy of the moment enveloping her. She reached out, her fingers lightly tracing the line of his jaw, the stubble from the night's growth tickling her skin. Taylor's eyes opened slowly, meeting Naomi's peaceful smile. There was no need for words; their shared look spoke volumes of the love and satisfaction they found in each other's presence. Taylor wrapped an arm around Naomi, pulling her close, their bodies fitting together like two pieces of a puzzle meant to be joined. The world outside continued to wake, but in their little sanctuary, time stood still. They lay there, in the soft embrace of the morning, the promise of the day ahead cradled in the tranquility of their arising.

Cassandra's deadline was a couple days away, so Naomi planned for her and Taylor to head back to Dallas as a show of support. Naomi ordered room service while Taylor showered. They enjoyed a light breakfast to get their day started. It was only 8:30 AM in San Diego, so Naomi would wait until later to call the agency in New Orleans due to the time difference. As Naomi headed to the bathroom, Lieutenant Augustine called with the latest information.

"Are you available to come down to the police station?" He asked Naomi, urgency was in his tone.

"Sure, I can head over there in ten minutes," she said, curious to what the information was.

"I am sending a car for you now," he told Naomi.

"Something urgent has come up, I need to go to the police department, Lieutenant Augustine has a car enroute to pick me up," Naomi informed Taylor.

"Do you need me to come with you?" Taylor asked.

"No baby, you stay back, and I will call you if I need you. I'll be back soon," Naomi told Taylor.

Naomi quickly dressed, then headed downstairs to the lobby as a black sedan pulled up to the hotel entrance. She made eye contact with the officer driving, who beckoned her with his hand. When they arrived at the police department Lieutenant Augustine and a female detective was waiting for her.

"This is Detective Yvonne Cato, she will fill you in," Lieutenant Augustine said, leading them both down a narrow hallway.

"You can call me Yvonne," she told Naomi, extending her hand.

"Thanks, and I am Naomi," she smiled, shaking her hand, nervously awaiting her response.

"We received a call around 4:00 AM from the hotel manager about a young lady found stumbling outside her hotel room. When they tried to assist, she became hysterical and combative," Yvonne said.

"Oh, my goodness," Naomi said, disturbed by this news.

"We were able to calm her down and brought her to the station. The Lieutenant asked me to wait on you to question Ms. Sanchez," Yvonne said, pointing to the closed door in front of them.

Detective Cato slowly opened the door to the interrogation room and introduced herself and Naomi. Naomi and Detective Cato sat across from the disheveled young woman in the San Diego police department's dimly lit interrogation room. The air smelled of stale coffee and apprehension. The woman's eyes were wide, pupils dilated, and her hands shivered as she gripped a used wrinkled tissue.

"Can I get you something to drink?" Detective Cato offered.

"No thank you," She responded softly.

"Ms. Sanchez," Naomi began, her voice calm but probing. "My name is Naomi Bloom, and I am a private investigator working with the San Diego police department. I know this is hard, but we need to figure out what happened last night."

Ms. Sanchez, a wealthy lawyer in her mid-thirties, took an uneasy breath. Her make-up was smudged, and her hair hung in tangled locs around her face.

"I... I don't remember much," she hesitated. "I went to the hotel bar with some people from the convention. We were celebrating a recent win I had in court that I shared with them."

Naomi leaned forward, pen ready over her notepad

"Did you have anything to drink?" Naomi asked.

Ms. Sanchez nodded. "Just one cocktail. But then everything got fuzzy. I remember talking, laughing, and then... nothing."

The detective's gaze never wavered. "Did anyone approach you? Maybe someone you didn't know?" Detective Cato asked.

Ms. Sanchez hesitated. "There was a man that joined our group who I remember seeing at the convention. Tall, dark hair. He seemed charming, but I can't recall much else," she told them.

Detective Cato jotted down notes. "Did he offer you another drink?"

"Yes," Ms. Sanchez whispered. "He insisted I try a special cocktail. Said it was his favorite."

"And after that?" Naomi chimed in.

"I felt dizzy and disoriented. The room spun. I remember stumbling a bit, and then... blackness."

Detective Cato's expression hardened. "Ms. Sanchez, we've seen cases like this before in the last few months. Date-rape drugs—GHB, Rohypnol, or ketamine—are often used to incapacitate victims. They leave you vulnerable, unable to resist."

Ms. Sanchez clenched her fists. "But why? Why would someone do this to me?"

The detective leaned back, her tone empathetic. "Sometimes it's about power, control. Other times, it's theft or worse. We're here to find out," Detective Cato explained.

Ms. Sanchez wiped tears from her cheeks. "I want justice. I want him caught."

Detective Cato nodded. "We'll do everything we can to catch him. But first, we need to run some tests. Collect evidence. And remember, Ms. Sanchez, you're not alone in this. We are here to support you."

"We believe you are not his only victim. Is there anything else you can remember to help us catch him?" Naomi added.

"Yes, I think I heard other voices, possibly a woman because I remember smelling Chanel perfume. I don't wear it because it gives me a headache," Ms. Sanchez recalled.

As the interview continued, Detective Cato's mind raced. Naomi wanted to share her thoughts about a potential serial predator, now there was the possibility of more than one suspect involved. Naomi had seen too many victims like Ms. Sanchez, strong, wealthy, women whose lives were shattered by a single drink. But this time, she vowed, they would catch the predator responsible. Justice would prevail, even in the gloomiest parts of the night.

Ms. Sanchez felt a mix of fear, confusion, and anger about her situation. Fear because she was uncertain about what happened during the blackout period, confusion because her memory was patchy, and anger because she was violated and demanded justice. She prayed that any test results would come back negative. Detective Cato arranged for a police officer to escort Ms. Sanchez to the hospital for the tests.

"Can Ms. Naomi come along with me?" Ms. Sanchez sheepishly asked the detective.

"That would be up to her, she is a consultant on this case," Detective Cato explained.

"I don't mind accompanying you," Naomi said quietly, gently touching her hand.

Naomi waited outside the exam room until the nurse gave the 'all clear' to enter. The sterile odor of disinfectant trailed in the air as Naomi stepped into the small, brightly lit examination room. The walls were basic white, with only a comprehensive anatomical diagram adding any trace of color. In the middle of the room sat a narrow examination table, its paper covering, ruffling under the weight of Ms. Sanchez. The nurse was an older woman with a gentle face and steady hands. Naomi watched as she methodically collected evidence from the assault. She spoke in hushed tones, offering words of comfort to Ms. Sanchez as she explained everything she was doing.

"Ms. Sanchez, I'm going to take a few photographs of your injuries now," the nurse said, her voice a blend of competence and compassion. The camera snapped, a dramatic sound in the quiet room, taking images that would serve as silent witnesses to the assault.

Naomi observed from a distance, her expression a mask of controlled rage and grief. She noted the precision with which the nurse worked, collecting samples with swabs, and sealing them meticulously for the crime lab. As the nurse continued her examination, Naomi made a silent vow to find the person responsible. The examination concluded with the nurse offering Ms. Sanchez a warm blanket and a cup of tea, her small acts of kindness an absolute contrast to the evil that had brought them all together in this room.

Naomi stepped forward, her voice gentle but firm. "Ms. Sanchez, when you're ready you can get dressed. I have a few questions that can help us catch whoever did this to you."

Ms. Sanchez nodded, a spark of resolve in her eyes. Naomi pulled up a chair, her notebook ready, attention fully on Ms. Sanchez.

"Did anyone else from your firm attend the convention?" Naomi asked.

"No, I attended the convention alone due to my trial running late," she confirmed.

"What type of convention and who was the host?" Naomi continued.

"It was a Continuing Legal Education convention hosted by Shamrock Legal Ed," she told Naomi.

"Who booked your trip?" Naomi asked. "I don't remember the agency, but I can have my secretary find out. Does she have to know what happened?" she asked, ashamed.

Fear gripped Ms. Sanchez as she thought about her colleagues finding out. She was now beginning to have hazy memories of that ominous night. The unknown terrified her—the gaps in her recollection, the vulnerability she felt, and the realization that someone violated her trust. Dread gnawed at her insides, leaving her on edge and fearful. She was experiencing a whirlwind of emotions and Naomi could see the anguish in her eyes, the same agony her friend Cassandra had experienced months earlier.

"Take your time Ms. Sanchez, just tell me anything you can remember no matter how trivial you may think it is," Naomi told her.

Ms. Sanchez relayed as much information as she could remember as snippets of her broken memories flashed through her mind. Her thoughts were a twisted jigsaw puzzle with so many fragmented sections. She strained to piece together the events leading up to her blackout. Why did she let her guard down and trust a stranger? What happened to her after the special cocktail? How did she get back to her hotel room? The confusion was frustrating, and she held on to Naomi's questions as a lifeline. Tears fell as she quietly spoke.

"I just can't believe my own words coming from my mouth," she sobbed, becoming angry.

Her anger simmered slowly beneath the surface. Anger at herself for letting her guard down. Anger at the predator who preyed on her defenselessness.

Naomi wanted justice, not just for Cassandra but for others who might have suffered the same fate, since she now suspected a serial predator. She clenched her fists and tightened her jaw as she vowed to fight back. Naomi had an increased need to catch this man. Her resolve hardened, she was determined that justice would prevail. Her agency would see to it.

"I promise you Ms. Sanchez that I will not stop until he is behind bars," Naomi said.

Cassandra Collins, Tanya Wilson, Cynthia Josephine, and Ms. Sanchez were all strong, independent women who attended conventions in their career fields, were the two things the victims had in common. In Ms. Sanchez's case, the perpetrator seemed to have escalated. He didn't stage anything, he actually assaulted her. The violation shattered dreams and her sense of safety. Naomi had her hands full with this case. The perpetrator was cold and calculated, adding to his list of crimes. Naomi was relieved Cassandra, and her family were in hiding but now Ms. Sanchez was on edge, terrified that her nightmare would be exposed to the world.

Chapter 10

Naomi and Taylor headed back to Dallas on an early morning flight. Today was the deadline for the extortion payout. The Dallas police carefully planned out their operation and coached a nervous Cassandra on what to say when the call came in. Like clockwork her phone rang at 11:30 AM with precise instructions on when and where to drop off the payment. Naomi was there to support her friend. She squeezed her hand as a sign of reassurance. The call only lasted a few seconds, which was not enough time for the police to attempt a trace. He was smart and arrogant, which only made Sergeant McLauglin more determined to catch him.

Her extortionist chose a public place and an evening time which would allow the police to get everything in place to catch him. Cassandra requested Naomi accompany the police to help ease her frazzled nerves. Naomi obliqued her friend and rode along with Sergeant McLaughlin to secure the area.

The sun was setting over Dallas, exposing the sky's hues of orange and pink as Cassandra stood in the crowded Klyde Warren Park, her heart beating inside her chest. She gripped her purse securely, the envelope filled with cash inside felt like it weighed a ton. She scanned the sea of faces, looking for the one that haunted her nightmares for weeks. Even though she did not know his true identity, just the thought of him being near her again terrified her.

The wait seemed endless, each minute felt like an agonizing hour. She felt unsettled and vulnerable, exposed and alone. Cassandra was paralyzed with fear as a man in a black hoodie separated himself from the shadows, his eyes hidden behind dark sunglasses despite the fading light. He approached Cassandra, his hand outstretched, palm up. She hesitated for a moment before placing the envelope in his hand. He wore dark glasses, and his face was shielded by the hoodie.

"The money is all here, just like you asked," Cassandra said nervously, her words measured and careful. "Now please, leave me and my family alone."

The man did not make a sound, nodded, turned, and disappeared into the crowd as quickly as he had appeared.

Cassandra tried to catch her breath, feeling a mixture of relief and fear. Cassandra noticed the two plainclothes detectives observing from a distance, their eyes tracking the extortionist as he quickly weaved through the park. They moved in to follow, but the park was bustling with families and street performers, making it extremely difficult to keep up, which it exactly what he planned. The suspect quicky turned a corner, and for a moment, he was out of sight. The detectives pushed through the crowd, but when they approached the spot where they last saw him, he was gone. They combed the streets frantically, radios buzzing with the voices of other officers joining the hunt, but it was as if the extortionist had vanished into thin air.

Back at the park, Cassandra was approached by Sergeant McLaughlin, who assured her they would not give up until the suspect was caught. But as she looked into the Sergeant's determined eyes, Cassandra couldn't shake off the feeling that the extortionist was far from done with her.

As night fell over Dallas, the city lights blinked on, and the extortionist watched from a distance, a sneer on his face. He had outmaneuvered the police once again, but he knew that the game was just beginning.

Cassandra was frazzled when they returned to the safe house.

"I can't let this man control my life! I thought we would have a fresh start," she cried.

"It's going to be ok," Charles promised.

Cassandra's husband tried to console her. Naomi stood helpless, her eyes met Taylor's in a silent plea to help her friend.

"Charles why don't you and your family come to New Orleans with Naomi and I," Taylor offered.

Naomi sighed as the words left his lips, confirming that Taylor was completely in tune with her thoughts.

"Would that be alright with you Sergeant?" Naomi asked.

"It actually may be the best thing for this family. They have already been through so much," he agreed.

Cassandra was overwhelmed with appreciation by the thoughtfulness of her friends. She graciously accepted their offer. Naomi hugged Taylor as the Collins family sought to close the door on this nightmare.

Taylor arranged a discrete transportation home to New Orleans. The sun was just dipping below the horizon, casting a warm golden glow over the Dallas skyline as Naomi stood on the tarmac, her eyes scanning the clear blue expanse above. She had made the call just hours earlier for Sergeant McLaughlin to bring Cassandra and her family to the designated hanger, and now, as the sleek private jet touched down, she felt a mixture of relief and anxiety.

"Are you sure this is safe?" Taylor asked, his voice barely audible over the roar of the engines.

"It's the only way," Naomi replied, her gaze never leaving the plane. "New Orleans is the best place for them right now and no one will be able to track where she is."

The pilot, a seasoned veteran with years of experience, stepped out of the cockpit and gave Naomi a reassuring nod.

"We'll get your friends there safely," he said, his voice firm and confident.

Naomi turned to Taylor, her eyes filled with gratitude.

"Thank you for doing this," she said. "I can't tell you how much it means to me."

Cassandra and her family arrived at the airport escorted by Dallas police, and one by one, they climbed the steps into the jet, their faces a mix of confusion and fear. Cassandra glanced back at the city they were leaving behind. As they settled into the plush leather seats, Cassandra took one final look at Dallas. She knew they were leaving a lot behind, but the safety of her family was all that mattered. With a gentle hum, the engines came to life, and the jet began to taxi down the runway. Cassandra held her breath as the jet picked up speed, the lights of the city blurring past the windows. And then, they were airborne, climbing higher and higher into the twilight sky. Cassandra felt relieved, feeling the weight of the world lifting from her shoulders.

"We'll be in New Orleans in no time," the pilot called over the intercom. "Sit back and relax."

Cassandra leaned back in her seat, she looked in Naomi's direction and felt relieved, closing her eyes. She didn't know what the future held, but for now, her family was safe. They were together and that was all that mattered. The plane touched down and the passengers departed. The car ride from the airport was quiet. They arrived home later than expected due to traffic and construction. Naomi opened the front door to their home, the scent of sweet jasmine spilled out into the cool night air. Taylor and Charles retrieved the luggage from the car, as Cassandra and her son followed behind Naomi, weary from their journey.

"Come in, come in," Naomi urged, stepping aside to allow them entry. "You're safe here," she smiled.

Cassandra's shoulders slumped with relief as she crossed the threshold, her son's hands tightly clasped in hers. Naomi led them into the living room so they could sit and relax. The men joined them shortly loaded down with luggage.

"Come on Charles, I will show you to the guest wing," Taylor motioned with his head for Charles to follow him.

Upstairs Taylor showed Charles around the guest wing to get him acquainted with his new surroundings. There was even an upstairs study available for him to work out of. Charles gave Taylor a firm handshake of appreciation. No words were needed.

"I can't thank you enough Naomi," Cassandra whispered, her voice thick with emotion. "We are beyond grateful."

"There's no need for thanks," Naomi replied, her tone gentle. "This is what friends are for. You and your family can stay here as long as you need."

Cassandra's son explored his new surroundings while Naomi and Cassandra sat down on the plush sofa in the den. They spoke in hushed tones, the gravity of the situation weighing heavily between them. Cassandra expressed how fortunate for her husband's job to be flexible with their situation.

Naomi listened as Cassandra recounted their stay in the safe house, the uneasiness she felt despite having so many police around, and the home they had been forced to leave behind once again. With each word, Naomi's resolve to protect them deepened.

"You'll have the guest wing upstairs," Naomi said, rising from the sofa. "There are two bedrooms and two bathrooms. And don't hesitate to use the kitchen. If you need anything special just make a list and we will take care of it. We have to get some fresh food in the house anyway since we have been busy traveling."

Cassandra nodded, her eyes filled with tears. "How can I ever repay you?" Cassandra asked.

Naomi smiled, placing a reassuring hand on her friend's shoulder.

"You don't owe me anything. Just focus on relaxing and spending time with your family. That's all the repayment I need," Naomi told her.

"Naomi, I just realized you are still newlyweds, and we are intruding, are you sure it's alright?" Cassandra asked.

"We would not have it any other way," Naomi assured her.

That night, as the house settled into a peaceful silence, Naomi lay awake, her thoughts on the family sleeping soundly under their roof. Taylor held her close reassuring her they made the correct decision. Naomi knew the road ahead would be filled with obstacles, but she was determined to provide a safe haven for Cassandra's family, a place where they could reclaim their lives, free from fear. In the safety of Naomi's home, Cassandra and her family found more than just sanctuary; they found hope, and the promise of a fresh start.

The first light of dawn had barely begun to seep through the curtains when Naomi's eyes flickered open. The house was silent, except for the soft, rhythmic breathing of her husband. She slipped out of bed, careful not to disturb his peaceful slumber. Walking softly downstairs and into the kitchen, Naomi flicked on the dimmest light, casting a warm glow over the marble countertops. Naomi reached for the bag of her favorite coffee beans, inhaling deeply as she poured them into the grinder. The low hum of the grinder broke the morning silence, a comforting sound that signaled the start of a new day. As the beans transformed into coarse grounds, Naomi couldn't help but smile at the familiar scent.

Next, she filled the kettle with water and set it to boil. While waiting, she pulled out her trusty French press, a cherished gift from her grandmother. It had seen many mornings like this, each one a blend of tranquility and anticipation.

With practiced precision, Naomi scooped the ground coffee into the French press, tapping it gently to level the surface. The kettle began to whistle, and she carefully poured the hot water over the grounds, watching as they bloomed and released their rich, earthy aroma.

Setting the timer for four minutes, Naomi took a moment to gaze out the window. The world outside was waking up, birds chirping and leaves rustling in the gentle breeze. She stirred the coffee, then placed the lid on the French press, the plunger pulled all the way up.

As the timer ticked down, she prepared two coffee mugs as usual. The timer chimed, and Naomi slowly pressed the plunger down, separating the fragrant coffee from the grounds.

Pouring the dark, steaming liquid into her mug, she savored the moment, taking a deep breath before taking her first sip. The warmth and richness of the coffee enveloped her senses, and she felt a sense of calm and contentment wash over her. Naomi leaned against the counter, cradling her mug in both hands, ready to face whatever the day might bring.

Next Naomi pulled out the ingredients for her famous pecan pancakes, the recipe a well-loved page in her grandmother's cookbook. The batter was mixed with a gentle hand, mindful not to overwork it, while the skillet warmed on the stove. She hummed a tune under her breath, a melody that spoke of comfort and the joy of caring for others.

As the pancakes cooked, she arranged the table with care—plates, flatware, and glasses all placed just so. A small vase of flowers picked from the garden added a splash of color to the scene. By the time the first pancake was ready to flip, she had finished her coffee. She smiled to herself, anticipating the surprise and delight of her friends as they awoke to the feast she was preparing.

The sun had fully risen by the time she heard the first stirrings from upstairs, Taylor was in the shower, no doubt he smelled the aroma of coffee. The kitchen was a symphony of scents and sounds, a testament to her early morning labor. Naomi placed the last pancake on the stack and turned to greet Taylor with a warm smile.

"Good morning!" Naomi said, full of enthusiasm, handing him a mug of coffee.

"How did you sleep?" Taylor asked, taking a drink from his mug.

"Surprisingly well after yesterday. I am so glad to be back home. Hotel living doesn't compare to your own home," Naomi said.

"Agreed and I think I hear some little feet shuffling around upstairs," Taylor laughed.

"Well, I figured we could all use a good breakfast to start the day," Naomi smiled, pointing to the stack of pancakes.

"What's the gameplan today?" He asked.

"Let's go in the office and try to make sense of everything so far. We can meet with the teams and see where they are. Plus, I think Cassandra and her family need some quiet time together," Naomi said.

"I completely agree with that. I am sure I have a ton of legal briefs to follow up on as well," Taylor told her.

"When she comes downstairs, I will show her where everything is then we can leave," Naomi confirmed.

They arrived at the agency shortly after 9:00 AM to find Margaret eagerly awaiting their return.

"Well, aren't the two of you a welcome sight," Margaret said.

"It's good to be back Margaret, but we have our work cut out for us," Naomi said, apprehensive.

"Whatever you need just let us know," Margaret said.

"Can you schedule a meeting for noon and order lunch for the office. I want to get everyone caught up on the case," Naomi said heading to her office. "And our client Cassandra and her family are in town staying with us," Naomi added.

Margaret followed Naomi to her office with an armload of mail and an ear ready for the details of how Cassandra ended up at their home.

"It's a long story Margaret, but the man who set Cassandra up for murder followed her to Dallas somehow and threatened her for more money. She was under police protection, but I felt it was best for her to leave. He won't be able to find her here," Naomi shared.

"That's so very considerate of you both, Naomi," Margaret smiled.

"She's had a rough year, and I feel a little guilty that our friendship ended how it did," Naomi said softly, taking a seat at her desk.

"Mrs. Collins was dealt a difficult hand, but I know this agency will help turn the bad around," Margaret said confidently.

"Definitely, I am ready to solve this case. First order of business is to create a profile on the suspect before the meeting," Naomi said.

"Ok I will leave you to it and set up the meeting, as well as lunch. Any preferences?" Margaret asked.

"As long as I can get a piece of bread pudding with lunch, you can pick the place," Naomi told her.

"I second that! And I need extra rum sauce," Taylor called out from his office.

Naomi worked throughout the morning sifting through every piece of information she obtained from Cassandra, both Dallas and San Diego police departments and the other victims. She combed through the video footage they obtained as well. She met with each team separately to review the information they compiled. Taylor brought her a hot chai latte along with the last of the files she requested from Margaret. He watched as she scoured over each document. He admired her dedication and tenacity. She worked right up until lunch gathering information to establish a profile on their suspect.

The **Secure Justice Agency** staff met in the large conference room for lunch and a meeting followed. After lunch Naomi presented the group with the profile of the suspect they sought.

"Our suspect preys on wealthy women attending business conferences alone. He is methodical, patient, and highly intelligent. He targets his victims with precision. He preys on their vulnerability, using charm and an appearance of empathy to gain their trust before he strikes."

"He befriends them, offers the unsuspecting victim a drink that he spikes. Once drugged, the women would wake to find themselves in a staged scenario, crafted to look like a scandalous affair or a compromising situation. The suspect would then extort money from them in exchange for his silence, playing on their fears of public disgrace and potential ruin of their reputations."

The team took notes as Naomi described in detail how she believed the suspect operated.

"I believe he is likely in his mid-30s to early 40s, someone who has experienced significant monetary loss, infidelity, and even abuse as a child. He has clear issue with women, maybe his mother abused him or neglected him in some way. He is familiar with the world of the elite, perhaps once a part of it himself, which would explain his ease in navigating their circles. He is educated and cunning. He is meticulous and calculated, always steps ahead of the police. Despite his charming exterior, he is cold and detached, viewing his victims as mere pawns in his twisted schemes."

"He is physically fit, able to overpower his victims quickly and efficiently. Most importantly, he is intensifying. With each attack, he becomes more brazen, more confident, and capable of murder. This is a man who believes he is untouchable, and that is what will ultimately lead to his capture. The missing component is how he locates his victims. I don't think he is working alone. He has been to conventions for bankers, realtors, and attorneys so far. We need to find out the common denominator here."

Naomi shuffled some papers and handed a copy of the suspect's profile to each of her staff.

"Wow Naomi, how'd you come up with all of that?" Taylor asked, impressed to see her mind in action.

"There is a science or technique to profiling I learned when I was with the DEA," Naomi shared.

Naomi now relied on her team to find the missing pieces. She assigned the surveillance team to obtain footage from each convention location to see if there were any guests fitting the suspect's description.

As Taylor and Naomi approached the front door of their home, the warm glow of the porch light welcomed them. The aroma of garlic and herbs wafted through the air, a fragrant promise of the feast that awaited them inside. Upon entering, they were greeted by the sight of their dining room transformed into a quaint Italian restaurant, complete with a red-and-white checkered tablecloth and flickering candles casting a soft light over the spread. At the heart of the table sat a rustic ceramic bowl brimming with fettuccini alfredo, its creamy sauce clinging to the twirls of pasta, punctuated by a generous amount of jumbo shrimp and a sprinkle of freshly grated Parmesan.

Cassandra emerged from the kitchen with a plate of freshly baked bread, her apron dusted with flour and a smile brightening her face.

"Welcome home!" she exclaimed, her hands gesturing towards the feast she had lovingly prepared. "I hope you're hungry. I've been cooking all day to make this dinner special for you two."

Taylor and Naomi exchanged a look of pleasant surprise and gratitude. They had expected to come home and order takeout since they would be traveling soon, but Cassandra had filled their home with the warmth of a family gathering. The table was adorned with side dishes, a caprese salad with ripe tomatoes and mozzarella, fried eggplant, and a bottle of Chianti that promised to complement the meal perfectly.

As they took their seats joined by Cassandra's husband and son, Cassandra poured wine for the adults, the ruby liquid sparkling in the candlelight. She then served them with the grace of a seasoned host, ensuring their plates were never empty and their glasses always full.

"Cassandra, you did not have to do all of this," Naomi said, marveling at the prepared feast.

"This is the least I can do Naomi, you and Taylor have made us feel so welcomed in your home," Cassandra smiled.

"Everything tastes wonderful," Taylor commented.

"I love the bread mommy," Brian said with his mouth full.

Charles smiled at his wife because he missed seeing her happy and right now her face beamed with pride from the compliments. It was a small slice of normalcy that had eluded them for so long. He could breathe easily as they took solace in a welcoming environment.

The evening culminated with a dessert of classic tiramisu, its layers of coffee-soaked ladyfingers and mascarpone cream, a sweet indication to the joy of unexpected pleasures. As they savored each bite, Taylor and Naomi knew that this was more than just a meal, it was a celebration of friendship, a sign of kindness, and a reminder that home is not just a place, but the people who fill it with love. Cassandra's gesture of preparing a homemade Italian dinner was not just about the food, but about recreating the bond that was broken.

Naomi helped Cassandra clear the dining table as the men retreated to the den with little Brian and Saint in tow. Taylor offered Charles a glass of whisky to cap off the wonderful meal. As the ladies worked restoring the kitchen to its original state they spent this time reconnecting.

"Naomi, I wasted our friendship with my own guilt and insecurities. I want you to know how genuinely sorry I am. I am forever in your debt for your hospitality towards me and my family. Brian is so content, he can be a child again and your puppy is just what he needs right now," Cassandra shared, through teary eyes.

"Cassandra, as difficult as your situation is right now, I believe it is proof to what true friendship is made of, supporting one another through life's challenges," Naomi said, holding both of her friends' hands.

"I have faith this will be over soon with your support," Cassandra said.

"Now let's go see what trouble these men are getting in," Naomi smiled.

The women rejoined their husbands as the men poured another round of whiskey. Naomi nestled beside Taylor seeking the familiar comfort and security he provided.

"Hey Brian, will you puppysit Saint while we are on our trip?" Naomi asked playfully.

"Yes, Miss Naomi I will," he said, beaming with joy, laughing as the puppy nipped at his fingers.

Cassandra smiled seeing her son's face light up, that alone erased any amount of trouble the family had faced. Charles could feel the tension ease in her body as she relaxed and enjoyed the rest of their evening.

"We are going to head up for the night, there's a lot of work to do," Naomi told her guests, reaching for her empty wine glass.

"I can take care of those," Cassandra said referring to their drink glasses.

"Thanks," Taylor smiled.

"Brian would you mind if Saint slept with you tonight to get accustomed to you," Naomi winked.

"Is that ok mom?" He squealed in a high-pitched voice.

"Of course, son, I'll tuck you both in," Cassandra said.

Cassandra hugged Naomi tightly as a show of gratitude.

Chapter 11

Naomi reached out to Lieutenant Augustine the next morning to update him on the latest findings of the investigation. **Secure Justice Agency** had an elaborate plan to catch their perpetrator who was still unidentified. The entire team headed to San Diego because she believed the upcoming pharmaceutical convention was the next plausible setting for him to strike based on his profile, because all of his victims attended a convention in San Diego. That was one of the common denominators of the victims, besides their wealth.

Naomi and her team, which consisted of herself, Taylor, Joseph Kensington, their surveillance expert, Anthony Wheaton, security expert, along with Oliver B. Young, their weapons/tech specialist, arrived two days prior to the pharmaceutical convention. Taylor strategically reserved 3 hotel suites under his law firm's name, 2 adjourning on either side of the center suite. Joseph and Oliver would outfit the room with surveillance equipment. Joseph began unpacking his gear: a sleek black case containing the latest in surveillance technology. First, they set up a tripod near the window, mounting a camera with a long-range lens capable of capturing the finest details from the suite next door. The camera, equipped with night vision and thermal imaging, would miss nothing, not even the subtlest of movements in the dead of night.

Next, Oliver installed a series of microphones along the shared wall, each one sensitive enough to pick up a whisper. The microphones were tucked within the lush carpeting, right against the shared wall, virtually undetectable. The microphones were connected to a sound amplifier and a set of high-definition headphones that would allow Joseph to listen in on even the most hushed conversations. The room was a technological network, with wires snaking across the floor, connecting to various devices that hummed with electricity. With expert hands, Joseph positioned a camera behind a tiny hole in the floral wallpaper, giving it an unobstructed view of the adjourning room through a similarly disguised hole. Several other cameras were strategically placed, their lenses peering through tiny holes drilled into the wall, giving Jospeh eyes throughout the entire suite next door.

On the desk, Joseph laid out a bank of monitors, each linked to cameras and microphones. He booted up a sophisticated facial recognition software that could identify suspects minutes after they stepped into view. The software was the latest from the FBI's tech division, capable of cross-referencing millions of faces in seconds. Finally, he pulled out his latest toy: a drone, no larger than a cell phone. This tiny marvel could slip under doors or through open windows, relaying live video feed directly to his monitors. It was silent, undetectable, and utterly indispensable for close-quarters surveillance.

With everything in place, Joseph dimmed the lights and settled into the plush armchair that faced the monitors. Headphones on, he watched and listened as Naomi walked into the suite next door to have them test out the equipment in place. The team sat quietly across the hall as Naomi moved throughout the suite to ensure they would be able to see and hear her every move. The final piece was simple, she hung the 'Do not disturb' sign on the door handle to the suite outfitted with equipment. Oliver would remain in the suite at all times. The trap was set, and now, all they needed was for their suspect to take the bait.

Naomi let herself into the opposite suite where she and Taylor were actually staying. She had to admit that she was nervous about their plan because they still did not have a name to their suspect, however Taylor produced an idea to identify every man that could potentially fit the profile. Joseph had a special app that he used to quickly run fingerprints through a vast database of suspects.

"Let's put Anthony in a role to capture fingerprints of male convention attendees," Taylor suggested.

"That's brilliant Taylor," Naomi beamed.

She was impressed by the amount of natural investigative insight he held. He was truly an asset to the agency.

"Well, we know he will be using a fake name, based on the other victim accounts," Naomi said.

"We're going to get him Naomi, I know it," Taylor assured her.

"San Diego police will have plain clothed officers throughout the convention, courtesy of Lieutenant Augustine. He's determined to get this guy off the street," Naomi said, rubbing her left temple.

"I can see the tension on your face, try to relax," Taylor told her.

"I am trying, but so much is depended upon our plan," Naomi said, worried.

Taylor moved toward her and gently pulled her towards him.

Her shoulders slumped, the weight of the world seemingly perched upon them. She exhaled a sigh that spoke volumes of her exhaustion. Without a word, he gestured towards the large armchair that sat invitingly by the desk.

"Come, sit," Taylor said, his voice soothing. "Let me help you unwind."

"So many things can go wrong," Naomi said.

"Everything will work according to our plans, believe in it and trust your instincts," he said.

Naomi managed a weary smile and sank into the chair, her head aching from the intensity of the investigation. Taylor stood behind her, his hands warm and steady. He began at the base of her neck, his fingers working gently but firmly, kneading away the knots of tension that had built up over the hours.

"You work too hard," he murmured, his thumbs pressing into the tender spots that made Naomi's breath hitch. "But right now, it's just you, me, and this moment of peace."

Naomi closed her eyes, letting the sound of Taylor's voice and the skill of his hands transport her away from the case. The pressure of his palms moved in rhythmic motions, tracing the lines of stress down her spine, dissipating them with every stroke. As Taylor's hands moved lower, easing the stiffness in her lower back, Naomi felt the day's worries melt away. The tightness in her chest loosened, her thoughts cleared, and for the first time all day, she felt like she could breathe again. Her body was free of tension and completely relaxed.

"Better?" Taylor asked, his hands coming to a rest on her shoulders.

"Much better," Naomi replied, her voice soft and content. "Thank you, my love."

"You know we are still newlyweds?" Taylor mused, turning her chair to face him.

"What about the team next door?" she asked, pointing to the wall.

"I already took care of that, the guys will be headed downstairs shortly for dinner," he proudly smiled.

"Seems like you planned this out in advance Mr. Sylvester," she jokingly admonished, shaking her finger at him.

"Room service is already on the way with our dinner," he informed her, leaning in for a kiss.

"You're the best, Taylor," she said, hugging his neck.

Naomi stood slowly into his awaiting embrace. He kissed her softly on her lips as the remaining tension evaporated. She closed her eyes as flashes of Fiji replaced her thoughts. She relinquished to his skillful touch as they silently moved towards the bed. Taylor was so powerful but gentle, the combination only intensified his passion for his wife. He lifted her small frame effortlessly as if she were a fragile trophy, but she was indeed his prized reward for which he cherished.

"Tell me what you want," he whispered in her ear.

Her response was interrupted by a knock at the door from the hotel attendant delivering their room service. Taylor quickly retrieved the table containing two silver domes that covered their dinner plates, an ice bucket with a chilled bottle of champagne and a large bouquet of fragrant flowers he had special ordered as a reminder of their honeymoon. He tipped the attendant and quickly closed the door behind him.

"Did you order appetizers?" Naomi smiled slyly, winking one eye.

"Should I have?" He wondered.

Naomi gestured for Taylor to come to her, and he obliged, carrying the flowers as their luscious scent trailed behind him.

"I didn't get a chance to tell you what I wanted," Naomi said as he came closer, resuming his place on the bed.

She whispered in his ear, and they shared a tender smile.

"Mrs. Sylvester, that I can definitely provide," Taylor said pulling a pink flower from the sweet bouquet.

He traced her soft jaw line and neck with the delicate flower, kissing each inch of the sweet trail it left behind. He used the flower as his guide to explore her body slowly, his private treasure. Dinner definitely would have to wait as they indulged in the appetizer course.

After a steamy shower, Naomi and Taylor enjoyed their reheated dinner and casual conversation in the stolen moment of time they shared. Naomi looked over at the rumpled sheets on the bed with flowers strewn about.

"I'm sure our housekeeper will have questions," she laughed.

"As your attorney, I advise you not to answer on the grounds I may be called as a corroborating witness," he smiled.

The two enjoyed a good long laugh at their flower playfulness. The rest of the team returned to the room next door. Taylor and Naomi joined them to review their plans for moving forward with their investigation.

"Thanks for dinner boss," Oliver said with a wide grin.

He was the youngest member of the agency but extremely skilled at his job. Oliver was eager and exited to be included in the team.

"You're welcome, Oliver," Taylor told him, shaking his hand.

"I love that tropical look on you Mrs. Sylvester," Oliver said gesturing to the flower stuck in her hair.

Naomi blushed as she touched her hair. "Oh yes, I just love flowers."

"Let's all get a good night sleep because we have an early morning of reconnaissance work tomorrow," Jospeh said.

"Yes definitely. Anthony and I will meet with Lieutenant Augustine tomorrow to discuss security," Naomi said in agreement.

"Have a good night team, I sincerely appreciate all of you," Taylor chimed in. "The goal is to catch a predator and murderer but most importantly we keep my wife safe."

"Of course," they all said in unison.

The next morning Naomi and Anthony met with Lieutenant Augustine at the San Diego police department as planned to inform him of everything her agency had in place. She shared their surveillance set up as well, since guests would begin arriving tomorrow for the start of the convention. Registration would take place throughout the day and there would be a happy hour mixer.

"I will have ten plain clothes police officers stationed at the convention and will have them meet your team to coordinate and introduce themselves. You can have them strategically placed throughout the convention center," Lieutenant Augustine informed Naomi.

"I appreciate your willingness to allow us to work with you. We need to catch him before he hurts anyone else because I fear he's spiraling," Naomi said worried.

"My officers will keep me informed, I don't want to chance him seeing me so I will be here at the station," he told Naomi.

Back at the hotel Naomi's team stayed out of sight in case the suspect was already at the hotel. They passed the time by double checking their plan and equipment. Room service would be their source of food for each meal during their stay in San Diego. Anthony started a friendly game of cards between the men, while Naomi caught up on her email messages from the agency. The men laughed, played 3 rounds of poker, and emptied the mini bar. Their voices resonated off the hotel room walls as the evening turned into night.

Naomi was ready to relax for the evening, so she excused herself.

"Make sure my husband gets home safely," she joked.

Taylor winked at Naomi as she exited the surveillance suite. Naomi went to their hotel room next door, took a long shower, and washed her hair. As she entered the bedroom area, Taylor opened the door.

"Oh my, I can smell that bourbon from here," Naomi said, fanning the air.

"Joseph spilled his glass on me after I beat him," Taylor laughed, removing his shirt.

"I need the team focused, I hope y'all didn't overdo it," Namoi said shaking her head.

"We are all sober, except for my clothes," Taylor smiled, walking towards Naomi swinging his shirt in her direction.

"Straight to the shower sir, you can't come to bed smelling like a distillery," Naomi insisted still waving her hands to fan away the intense smell of bourbon.

Taylor obliged his wife and showered before retiring for the night. His freshly showered body was warm and inviting. She snuggled next to him enjoying his scent. Taylor pulled Naomi close to him as they drifted off into a restful sleep.

Under the bright lights of the convention center, Naomi checked in at the reservation desk. She adjusted her glasses and smoothed out her business suit as she looked at her surroundings. She was no longer an investigator for the evening; she was 'Janet Bradshaw,' a pharmaceutical researcher from Miami. The first evening was a happy hour mixer, meet and greet event. Anthony was in place posing as a bartender to monitor drinks provided to any women at the convention, his keen eyes missing nothing. Anthony was also set up to retrieve fingerprints left on drink glasses by men. Taylor was also in place as a pharmaceutical sales representative, so he was a set of additional eyes. He scanned the crowd, keeping a close watch on Naomi.

Naomi took a seat at the bar, her demeanor calm but her senses on high alert. She ordered a drink, her voice steady, giving nothing away. Anthony nodded subtly in acknowledgment, sliding a glass towards her with practiced ease. They had to be careful; one wrong move could spook their suspect. Taylor took a seat next to Naomi and ordered a whisky. The two made brief eye contact but did not want to appear to know each other. As the night wore on, Naomi observed the convention attendees, her trained eye making mental notes to pick up on any subtle cues of discomfort and coercion.

Naomi had studied his profile they created, and as she surveyed the convention center, she spotted a possible suspect with a charming smile and a predatory gaze, moving through the convention hall. He made his way to the bar area and approached a young woman sitting nearby. She felt a chill as he approached the bar area, his smile never reaching her eyes. Naomi could not get a clear look at him without being too obvious.

"What's a beautiful woman like you doing all alone?" Naomi heard him ask a young woman near her, his voice smooth as silk.

The young woman smiled, "Just enjoying the music," she replied, her tone light. "And the company, it seems," she said smugly.

Naomi's eyes fixed on the suspect, trying to make out the name on his ID badge. Anthony carefully watched their interaction, the listening device he installed under the bar transmitted their conversation back to the surveillance suite. Oliver listened in as the two strangers spoke.

He asked many probing questions sizing up a potential target. Her name was Terez, she was from Savannah and was an assistant to one of the pharmaceutical representatives who paid for her to attend the convention for her continuing education. The suspect seemed no longer interested in her, politely excusing himself. He left the bar area and disappeared from the convention area. Naomi and her team along with the plain clothes officers scanned the area but he slipped away from them. At least they knew what he looked like thanks to the mini camera made to resemble a button on Anthony's shirt.

Anthony carefully removed the glass filled with wine he poured earlier for their prime suspect to test for fingerprints.

"Gotcha," he murmured, pulling a compact fingerprint kit from his leather satchel.

He quickly dusted the rim carefully with fine, black powder, his hand steady despite the adrenaline coursing through his veins. As the dust adhered to the oils left behind, a whirl of loops and swirls began to form. With practiced skill, Anthony applied a strip of clear adhesive tape over the print, sealing the suspect's fate along with it. He carefully lifted the tape, now carrying the crucial evidence, and placed it onto a plastic card. He would need to scan the fingerprint back at their surveillance suite. Anthony signaled one of the undercover officers posing as another bartender to replace him as he discretely made his way up to the surveillance suite. Naomi kept a close eye on the room to make sure their target did not return. She retreated to their surveillance room, followed by Taylor shortly after.

Anthony was already processing the fingerprint.

sample when Naomi quietly entered the room. They all stood in silence as the phone app searched through its vast database. As the minutes passed, it seemed as if the team held their breath as a collective until a series of beeps cut through the silence. Their suspect had a name now. The fingerprint was a match for Maurice Jeffrey. Anthony alerted Lieutenant Augustine who was on standby to do a more thorough check.

"We are so close to catching this creep, I can just feel it," Naomi said, her voice filled with confidence.

"I am ready for this to be over," Taylor chimed in.

"But we need compelling evidence to put him away for good, not just his fingerprint and the hazy memories of his victims. We need to catch him in the act," Naomi said.

"This plan of yours better work," Taylor said.

"It will," Naomi told him.

After what seemed like hours, Lieutenant Augustine finally called Anthony back. Anthony placed the call on the speakerphone.

"Go ahead Lieutenant, we are all here," Anthony said.

"This guy we are after has quiet an extensive record in Chicago. I was able to call in a few favors to get as much as I could," sharing what he found.

"Maurice Jeffrey grew up in the shadow of wealth, his father was a disgraced former investment banker who had lost their fortune in a high-stakes scandal. His mother divorced his father, leaving her family due to the shame his father brought to the family name. He was raised in a world of privilege he could no longer access, so he developed a deep resentment for the elite society that had shunned his family. He was intellectual and charming, traits that he learned to weaponize at an early age."

"His first venture into crime was as a con artist, running small scams that preyed on the vulnerabilities of the wealthy. However, he quickly escalated to more lucrative endeavors. He became a master of manipulation, using his charm to gain the trust of wealthy women before blackmailing them with secrets he meticulously uncovered. His operations were sophisticated, involving fake identities, psychological profiling, and a network of informants who helped him gather compromising information."

"His method was always the same. He would infiltrate high society events or professional conventions, often posing as a wealthy entrepreneur or investor. He would target lonely, often neglected wives of powerful men, wooing them with attention and promises of discretion. Once he had gained their trust, he would spike their drink and access to their private lives, he would uncover or fabricate incriminating evidence, then threaten to expose them unless they paid him off."

"For years, Jeffery evaded capture by moving from city to city, leaving a trail of shattered lives in his wake. This is the closest anyone has come to catching him. Naomi, I must commend you and your agency," Lieutenant Augustine told her.

"Your officers have his photo to monitor for any movements, but I want to stick to our original plan, using me as bait," Naomi said, looking in Taylor's direction.

Taylor hated having his wife in harm's way, but he had faith in her and his friends to keep her safe. He watched her with a mix of admiration and fear. Admiration for the strength she possessed, the same strength that had drawn him to her all those years ago. Fear for the unknown, for the possibility that each kiss, each touch, each goodbye could be their last.

"Be careful," Taylor finally said, his voice barely above a whisper. It was all he could manage without letting the dam break, without letting her see the depth of his worry.

Naomi walked over, her steps resolute. She knelt before him, taking his hands in hers, her touch warm and reassuring, "I will," she promised, her eyes locking onto his with an intensity that left no room for doubt. "I always am."

Chapter 12

Naomi's 3-inch heels clicked against the marble floor as she headed toward the hotel bar, a rhythmic echo that matched the steady beat of her heart. Her eyes were sharp, scanning the room with ease. She settled at the bar, the light fabric of her dress whispering against the stool as she took her seat. The dress she wore hugged her shapely frame with sophistication.

The bartender, Anthony, offered a nod and a smile, sliding a menu towards her. "What can I get for you, miss?"

"Just a club soda, thank you," Naomi replied, her voice low but clear. She wasn't here for the drinks.

As Anthony turned away, Naomi's gaze fixed on the mirror behind the bar, giving her a perfect view of convention attendees. She was looking for one man in particular, their suspect, Maurice Jeffrey.

As the minutes ticked by, each one seemed to stretch longer than the last. Then, there he was, entering through the double doors, his suit perfectly tailored. He approached the bar, unaware of the trap laid out for him. Naomi turned, offering a smile as warm as the whiskey he ordered. "Is this seat taken?" she asked, gesturing to the stool beside him.

The suspect's eyes flickered with interest. "For you? It's available."

She could not put her finger on it, but something was different about him that she had not noticed yesterday. His eyes seemed gentler, younger even.

"How are you enjoying the convention so far?" He asked.

"It is a bit boring," Naomi told him.

"Really, I was thinking the same thing," he smiled.

"I'm Janet Bradshaw by the way," she said, gesturing to her name badge.

"Oh, I left my badge in the room, my name is Dr. Raymond Hales," he said.

"Nice to meet you Dr. Hales, where are you from?" she asked.

"Los Angeles," he told her.

"I've never been there," she said, trying to make generic conversation.

"And what do you do Janet Bradshaw?" he asked, checking his phone as if disinterested.

"It's Dr. Bradshaw," she corrected him. "I'm a chemist and owner of a cosmetic company," she bragged, seeming to draw his attention again.

"Quite incidentally I am a cosmetic surgeon here to learn about the latest drug therapy for scarring," he told her.

Naomi was somewhat impressed with the lengths Jeffrey went through to come across as convincing. As they spoke, Anthony texted the name he provided to the San Diego police for them to run a background check. As expected, the alias Jeffrey used did not exist anywhere, but even more disturbing, someone presented themselves to the hotel concierge as Janet Bradshaw requesting a replacement room key from the plain clothed officer working at the hotel desk. The officer obliged them, so as not to alert the imposter.

Anthony notified the team as to what transpired. Soon after Oliver observed the imposter enter the room that was outfitted with cameras and listening devices. The woman searched carefully for valuables to find designer dresses in the closet along with jewelry in a small bag inside a suitcase. Jeffrey was not working alone, he had a female accomplice. Oliver snapped photos of the female as she continued to search the room. Their surveillance equipment was securely hidden and was able to capture everything.

Oliver texted Taylor and Anthony alerting them as to what was happening. Taylor immediately returned to the surveillance suite and could not believe what he was witnessing.

"Well, I'll be damned!" Taylor said.

"Naomi is his next target for sure," Oliver said.

"I'm headed to the bar to watch this prick," Taylor said angrily.

"I've already alerted Anthony," Oliver reassured Taylor.

"Naomi needs me," he said heading to the door.

"Are we going to let this play out?" Oliver asked.

"I don't want to, but I will go and warn Naomi. You watch the room and keep me updated," Taylor said.

Taylor messaged Anthony to notify him that Naomi had indeed been singled out as the next victim for Jeffrey and as Naomi suspected he was not working alone. Anthony activated the recording device at the bar but wasn't able to signal Naomi instead he alerted Taylor who made his way back downstairs.

At the bar area Naomi continued her conversation with Jeffrey as Taylor approached. He took an empty seat near her, dropping his phone to grab her attention. Taylor thought of an inconspicuous way to inform her that something was wrong.

"I'll have a vodka martini," Taylor stated, ordering a drink Naomi knew he hated.

Naomi's eyes widened, putting her on high alert.

Oliver messaged Taylor and Anthony to advise them that the woman searching Naomi's hotel suite left but he did not know where she went.

Jeffrey checked his phone and seemed to be pleased with what he saw because he had a slick smirk on his face.

"All ok Dr. Hales?" Naomi asked.

"Yes Dr. Bradshaw, can I get you another drink," He offered.

"Sure, a rum punch would be great," she said.

Jeffrey placed the drink order with the bartender 'Anthony.' Anthony prepared two rum punch drinks, along with a scotch on the rocks.

Naomi excused herself, feigning at trip to the bathroom. Like clockwork, Jeffrey quickly slipped a substance into Naomi's drink but as he looked away momentarily Anthony swapped out the drink for Naomi. Jeffrey also did not pay attention to Taylor leaving the bar.

Taylor and Naomi slipped away to a secluded area near the bathroom.

"You were right Naomi, he does have an accomplice. A woman accessed and searched your room so I can only imagine what she was looking for," Taylor informed her.

"He must have received the message from her because he seemed pleased and then offered to get me another drink," Naomi said.

Taylor's phone buzzed as Naomi spoke.

"He's making his move on you for sure, Anthony witnessed him spike your drink but was able to swap it out," Taylor said with relief in his voice.

"I need to get back and will have him believe I am under the influence of the drug," Naomi said.

"I will keep you safe," Taylor said, anxiously wanting to hold her but he could not risk it.

Naomi returned to the bar area, apologizing for the delay.

"Sorry it took me so long, I received a call from my company that I needed to take care of something urgently," she explained.

"I completely understand. Let's toast to putting out fires," he suggested with a slick smile, handing her the glass of rum punch.

"Definitely," she said, taking a long drink from the glass.

"I am never able to finish an entire convention in peace, always something to handle back at my practice," he said, keeping up his ruse.

"This is a good drink, bartender," Naomi commented, signaling Anthony as she continued to drink from the glass.

Anthony watched as Naomi faked a reaction of being drugged.

"Ma'am, are you alright?" the bartender, Anthony asked.

"I... I don't feel so good," Naomi whispered.

"I'm a doctor, I can take care of my friend. I will just help her to her room," he said, conveniently knocking over her drink to conceal having spiked the glass.

Jeffrey waved to a nearby female hotel employee, as Taylor watched from a distance, the same women who was in Naomi's room earlier came to assist him. Their malevolent plan was underway. Taylor contacted Lieutenant Augustine to have his officers on standby as he hurried back to the surveillance room joined by one of the police officers so as to observe what would transpire.

Anthony remained in place at the bar area until the police could come to retrieve the evidence Jeffrey left behind. The hotel lobby was intentionally quiet, with mostly staged police officers in place as convention attendees. The hotel manager glanced up from his desk with a concerned expression. Jeffrey offered a slight smile and head gesture, their silent exchange acknowledging the situation without a word being spoken. Jeffrey took the elevator up to the correct floor and made his way with Naomi to her hotel suite with the aid of his unidentified accomplice. The woman retrieved the room key from her pocket, opening the door.

Surveillance video captured the criminal duo entering the room struggling with Naomi as she pretended to be in and out of consciousness, making it as difficult as possible for them to maneuver her body. Jeffrey was too strong for Naomi as he picked her up, placing her on the bed. The female accomplice removed Naomi's shoes, placing them near the end of the bed.

"Remove her clothes and lay them out as usual," Jeffrey told the woman.

The woman attempted to remove Naomi's jacket, but she groaned loudly startling the woman.

"I think she's waking up like the other lady did," the women said nervously.

"I'll take care of that," Jeffrey said, removing a syringe from his coat pocket.

On the other side of the wall, Taylor had seen enough. He refused to put Naomi in any further danger.

"Is that enough evidence to put this guy away?" Taylor asked the police officer.

"Since we don't know what he has in that syringe I agree with making entry," The officer said.

"Let's go," Taylor said, in agreement with that assessment, Taylor handing him the spare room key.

The officer quickly opened the door with his weapon drawn.

"Drop the syringe, you're under arrest," The officer ordered.

"What are you doing? I am a doctor and was asked to assist the woman by the hotel," he said as if he had his alibi rehearsed.

"Step away from her until we sort things out," the officer said firmly.

"You can ask this hotel employee," he insisted.

"I am taking you both in custody, drop the syringe and put your hands behind your back. You as well young lady, hands behind your back and step away from the bed," the officer ordered.

Jeffrey's thoughts raced, he was cornered and had no escape. He had to think quickly to make a run for it. He grabbed his accomplice and held the syringe to her neck in an attempt to make the police stand down. Taylor was outside the door, impatiently waiting to make an entry. The woman struggled to get free as the police officer tried to get him to surrender. His eyes were wild, darting between the door and the woman he held close, a human shield against the inevitable. Jeffrey backed further into the large room toward the window. Naomi took this as an opportunity to 'awaken' from the spiked drink. She could tell by the officer's voice where he was standing in respect of the positioning of the bed. She made a hasty move, leaping to her feet, catching Jeffrey off guard.

"What is going on here?" Naomi said as she headed to the officer.

"Get back here!" Jeffrey yelled.

Naomi looked back at Jeffrey but proceeded to exit the room, leaving him to deal with the police.

Naomi went toward the sound of Taylor's voice as she heard him calling her name.

"No more undercover work for you," he said pulling her into the safety of his arms.

She nodded her head in agreement. They rejoined their surveillance team as the police were now in charge of the situation. As they watched the events play out from the other room, the woman's breaths came in short, sharp gasps, her eyes wide with terror. She tried to steady her trembling hands, to show no fear, but the sharp point of the needle at her throat made her panic.

Outside, the corridor was now lined with officers in tactical gear, their weapons trained on the door. The lead negotiator, a man with years etched into his face and a voice that had talked down the edge of many a cliff, spoke through the megaphone.

"This doesn't have to end badly," he called out, his words measured and calm. "Let her go, and we can talk this through."

But the suspect was beyond reason, past bargaining. He shouted back, a string of demands and curses that echoed off the walls. The tension was a tangible thing, a living entity that filled the space with its oppressive weight.

Suddenly, the suspect's demands ceased, and for a moment, there was silence—a brief, haunting calm in the storm. Then, without warning, the door burst open, and the room erupted into a frenzy of motion. Officers poured in, their shouts merging into a discord of sound. The suspect spun, his grip on the woman tightening, but she seized the moment, her survival instincts kicking in. With a swift, desperate move, she stomped on his foot and elbowed him in the stomach.

The syringe clattered to the ground as the suspect doubled over, and the woman broke free, scrambling away from his grasp. The officers were upon him in an instant, tackling him to the ground, their commands barked with military precision. Handcuffs clicked shut, and the suspect was dragged away, his shouts dwindling in the distance. The woman, now safe, was handcuffed as well until the police could make sense of what occurred.

Chapter 13

Lieutenant Augustine was now on the scene trying to make sense of the events that transpired.

"I received a call from the hotel reporting that a guest had been attacked in room 1022," he told Naomi.

"That's not my room number and we didn't contact the hotel, only your department was aware about the operation," Naomi said, confused by his statement.

"Let me radio the station to confirm," he told Namoi.

"Dispatch this is Lieutenant Augustine, please confirm 10-32 call."

"10-32 at your location, female victim, last name Andrews, room 1022," The voice called back

"What?" Naomi wondered aloud, completely off guard.

"Where is the victim?" Augustine asked.

"Still on location," the dispatcher said.

"Can we go speak to her?" Naomi asked.

The hotel room was dimly lit, the curtains fluttered slightly as the air conditioning hummed in the background. Naomi and Lieutenant Augustine stood in the center of the room, their expressions solemn. Across from them sat Sabrina Andrews, a young woman in her mid-twenties, wrapped in a hotel robe, her eyes red-rimmed but intense.

Naomi began gently, "Miss Andrews, we know this is difficult, but we need to understand what happened. Can you tell us about the events leading up to the assault?"

Sabrina took a deep breath, steadying herself.

"I was at the bar downstairs, just having a drink after the conference. He... he seemed nice at first, offered to buy me a drink," Sabrina Andrews said.

"Did you notice anything unusual about him? Anything at all that stood out?" Lieutenant Augustine asked.

Sabrina paused, thinking.

"Not really, just... just that he was very insistent on which drink I should try. I didn't think much of it then," Sabrina Andrews said.

Augustine scribbled something on his notepad.

"And then what happened?" Naomi asked.

Sabrina Andrews continued, "We talked for a bit, and then I started feeling dizzy. I excused myself to come up to my room, and he offered to help me..."

Her voice trailed off, and she shuddered from the thought of what had happened.

"It's okay, Sabrina. Take your time. We're here to help you," Lieutenant Augustine said.

Sabrina nodded, gathering strength from Detective Augustine's reassuring tone.

"The next thing I remember, I woke up here, feeling... wrong. I knew something had happened. I was scared and alone," Sabrina Andrews continued to recount.

Naomi reached out and placed a comforting hand on Sabrina's shoulder.

"You did the right thing calling the police, Sabrina. We're going to do everything we can to catch the person responsible," Naomi reassured her.

Sabrina looked up with a determined flash in her eyes.

"I want to help. I don't want this to happen to anyone else," Sabrina told them.

Naomi and Lieutenant Augustine exchanged a look of shared resolve.

"We'll need you to try and remember any details, no matter how small. We'll catch him, Sabrina. We promise," Lieutenant Augustine said.

"One more thing Sabrina, could you recall what he looked like if we showed you a picture of the suspect?" Naomi asked, looking at her phone.

"You have a picture of him?" she asked, a hint of fear in her tone.

"Our surveillance cameras may have picked up something?" Naomi said, standing and looking at the Lieutenant.

"One moment Sabrina, we will be right back," Lieutenant Augustine said, as he walked towards the door.

They both stepped outside the hotel room, closing the door behind them.

"What pictures?" Augustine asked.

"When I first profiled Maurice Jeffrey, I had this feeling he was not working alone but now I am sure of it. I think we've stumbled across some type of sadistic and twisted extortion ring with multiple suspects," Naomi shared.

"Are you sure?" Augustine asked with hesitation.

"Yes, when I was at the bar, I initially observed who I thought was Jeffrey sizing up a potential victim. She didn't meet his expectations, and he seemed annoyed and moved on. Anthony took pictures of him but the encounter I had with the man your police have in custody had a different demeanor. He seemed more refined, poised even. I think we are dealing with two different people, relatives, or brothers even," Naomi tried explaining.

"You're kidding me, right?" He said sarcastically.

"I wish I was, but that wasn't Maurice who was taken into custody," Naomi said.

She had Anthony send her the pictures he had taken at the bar, along with pictures of her team.

"I'll show her 5 pictures and let her determine who she encountered," she told Augustine, flipping through the pictures on her phone.

Lieutenant Augustine looked at the pictures of the suspects and he could definitely see a distinct difference. He could not believe it, but Naomi was right. They returned to the hotel room to speak with Sabrina.

"Miss Andrews, take your time and look at each picture carefully," Augustine coached.

Sabrina flipped through each picture multiple times looking intensely at the phone screen. She kept going back and forth between two pictures as Naomi and Lieutenant Augustine looked on.

"I can't be certain, but I think it's this man, or maybe this one," she said confused, unsure with her selection.

"You're doing great," Naomi encouraged her.

"We'll have an officer take you to the hospital, if you can quickly get dressed and unfortunately you can't shower," Augustine informed her.

"Can you take me?" Sabrina asked softly.

Naomi looked at Lieutenant Augustine for approval.

"Of course she can, she will ride with you in the police car," he confirmed.

Sabrina went to the bathroom to prepare to leave as Naomi messaged her team with updates.

"If you are correct Naomi, we have two suspects at large. We will run prints of the two we have in custody. Neither have said anything," Augustine shared.

"I think we need to start from the beginning to see what we missed. We need to show photos to all of the victims, including a photo of 'Sebastian Daniels.' I feel he was somehow involved as well. We also need to get as much hotel security footage as possible," Naomi said.

"Maybe once they get to the police station, reality will hit them. I would suggest trying to get the woman to talk and use the fact that he was willing to harm her to save himself," Augustine said.

The car ride to the hospital was painfully silent. A female officer accompanied Naomi and the victim.

It was like déjà vu as Naomi waited outside the exam room, the sterile odor of disinfectant reminiscent in the air as Naomi stepped into the small, brightly lit examination room. These same walls held the secrets of woman who were exposed and vulnerable. Sabrina sat on the exam table trying to remain composed but the paper covering ruffled under her legs. The nurse entered the room and carefully explained what needed to be done during the exam. She apologized to Sabrina in advance.

Naomi had Sabrina pack a change of clothing so she could take a shower once the exam was concluded and accompanied her back to the hotel.

"Would you be able to come back to my room, I don't want to be alone," she pleaded.

Naomi could not say no to her request seeing the helplessness in her eyes.

"I will," Naomi said gently.

"I appreciate it," Sabrina told her.

"Do you live in San Diego? Do you have any family we can call?" Naomi asked.

"No, I live in Detroit and it's just me and my mom," Sabrina shared.

Naomi's heart ached for Sabrina, her pain was palpable. She tried to keep the conversation light until they returned to the hotel. Naomi gave the small bag given to her by the nurse to Lieutenant Augustine for evidence.

"I'll make sure she gets checked out of the hotel and my agency will take care of her return home," Naomi informed Lieutenant Augustine.

He appreciated Naomi's concern and new insight in the investigation.

"We would not have gotten this far without your detective agency," he said sincerely.

Naomi provided Sabrina with her contact information and offered to keep her informed with the ongoing investigation concerning her. She did not disclose any information regarding the previous cases.

Naomi was able to secure a flight back to Detroit for Sabrina and because the San Diego airport was a short distance from the hotel Naomi accompanied Sabrina to the airport and back.

She felt sorrowful leaving her alone under the circumstances but the best place for her would be back home.

Naomi and her team, along with Lieutenant Augustine reconvened in their makeshift command center. Anthony and Oliver played all of the surveillance footage they were able to capture. Lieutenant Augustine planned to prepare a search warrant to obtain hotel security video. He watched as the woman they had in custody searched Naomi's room, pocketing various valuable items she found, looking through the closet and sizing up the clothing inside.

"She has indeed done this before," Taylor commented.

"If she has any of those items on her we can add that to her charges," Lieutenant Augustine said.

"Tomorrow let's sort some of this out, we need to speak with all of the victims and have them look at some photos," Naomi said.

Lieutenant Augustine contacted the four assault victims involved in their assault and extortion case. He debated whether to have them all appear at the same time, maybe solidarity would prove helpful knowing they were not alone. He took the chance and had them show up at the same time. Naomi was waiting in a large conference room as each woman walked in one by one, her presence was a calming sight. Lieutenant Augustine was the last to enter the room, closing the door behind him.

"Good morning ladies, thank you all for meeting here on such short notice but I promised to keep you informed in your case," he began.

"Each of you have met with Naomi Bloom on separate occasions but we thought it necessary for you to meet each other because we believe all of your cases are connected to a case that led Naomi here. Two women will be joining via phone, Cassandra Collins, and Christina Sanchez," he continued.

Naomi pressed the button on the conference phone and after a few clicks to signal the calls were connected she began.

"Sabrina Andrews, Tanya Wilson, meet Cynthia Josephine," Naomi said, signaling out each woman as she mentioned their name, "and on the phone we have Christina Sanchez and Cassandra Collins. I will be completely transparent and blunt. This case began with my old friend Cassandra Collins, who contacted me to help clear her name of a murder she did not commit. Cassandra, like each of you here attended a business conference in San Diego. She met a charming stranger at the conference, shared a few conversations, he befriended her and once he had gained her confidence they shared drinks. Her drink was laced with an unknown substance and her next memory was waking up in her hotel room."

Naomi surveyed the room for any type of response, but each woman present sat attentively listening. Naomi could also hear the faint sound of sobbing over the intercom, which she knew was coming from Christina Sanchez, the youngest and latest victim.

"A demand for money of some sort accompanied by incriminating photos would follow. In Cassandra's case she was linked to a murder that is still under investigation, but she was cleared."

Naomi looked to Lieutenant Augustine to see if he wanted to chime in. He nodded his head as if to say, 'good job, keep going.'

"We currently have a suspect in custody, but we need to make a positive identification first. We will show you all pictures to view to see if you can identify the person. I have emailed these same pictures to Casaandra and Christina."

Lieutenant Augustine spread the photographs across the wooden table with a practiced flick of his wrist. The air thick with tension as the women seemed to hold their collective breath.

"Take your time," Lieutenant Augustine softly instructed.

Tanya sat across from him, her hands trembling slightly as she reached for the first photo.

The images were a blur of faces for her, but Tanya's eyes were searching for one in particular. She shuffled through them methodically, her breath hitching every time a pair of eyes seemed to stare back with malice.

Then she stopped. Her hand hovered over a photo, and she felt a cold shiver run down her spine. It was him. The sharp jawline, the piercing dark eyes, even the smug tilt of his lips—it was the face that had haunted her dreams.

"That's him," Tanya whispered, her voice barely audible. "That's the man who attacked me."

Lieutenant Augustine's eyes hardened as he followed her gaze.

"Are you sure?" he asked, his voice steady.

Tanya nodded, her fingers tracing the outline of the face in the photo.

"I'll never forget those eyes," she said, a mixture of fear and resolve in her voice.

Naomi marked the back of the photo with Tanya's initials in tiny black letters. Mrs. Josephine looked through the photos carefully and to Naomi's surprise she picked out an unexpected photo. And as before Naomi placed Mrs. Josephine's initials on the back of the photo she selected. Sabrina looked through the same group of photos, selecting a different person from the other two women. Like the other two times, Naomi marked this photo as well. Naomi instructed Cassandra and Christina to reply to the email with their suspect selection and each time her phone chimed with a new email response Naomi marked the appropriate photo.

"We thank each of you for coming in and you have been brave throughout your ordeal, but I see strength in each one of you and I will be available for anything you need. I plan to see this case until the end to make sure each of you get the closure and justice you deserve," Naomi said committed to each woman.

As the women left the conference room, Naomi gave them her personal contact information, emphasizing her availability. Lieutenant Augustine could tell by Naomi's pensive expression she had information to share with him.

"Cynthia Josephine picked out 'Sebastain Daniels,' the man Cassandra Collins supposedly killed," Naomi said.

"What is going on here?" Lieutenant Augustine said scratching his head.

"We need to speak with the two you have in custody if you we allow me to sit in and ask a few questions," Naomi said.

"I definitely want you in the room," He agreed.

"We should speak to the female first. Did her fingerprints come back yet?" Naomi asked.

"She's not in our system, but I am sure your team may have other resources, so I sent a copy to Anthony. He said he should have something soon," Augustine told Naomi.

"I rather wait to know who she is before we go question her. How long can you hold her before charging her?" Naomi asked Lieutenant Augustine.

"72 hours but we are definitely charging her," he said emphatically.

"I have a few leads I am working on so let's reconvene in a few hours," Naomi said.

Naomi returned to the hotel and looped her team in on what occurred at the police station. She also returned Margaret Regis' phone call which filled in much needed gaps in the case.

"We found two sealed juvenile records that are linked to Maurice Jeffrey," Margaret shared.

"Please send them over and I'll have Taylor work on them," Naomi told Margaret.

"And one other thing, Cassandra found a cryptic email in her spam folder that is a few months old that she thought you might want to see," Margaret shared.

"Yes, please send that as well," Naomi instructed.

The team was in full swing tracking down all new leads and reviewing their old records.

Anthony was working on establishing the identity of the female suspect that was apprehended. He had special clearance in his line of work, giving him access to several databases. He sat hunched over his laptop clicking keys and checking his cellphone. After a series of beeps from his laptop, he muttered, "Gotcha."

"Meet Megan Young," Anthony said proudly, mirroring his laptop screen on the large monitor on the desk beside him for the team to see.

"She was born Megan Jeffrey then changed her last name ten years ago to Young. I searched for Megan Jeffrey, and she has a juvey record that I am working to unseal," Anthony said.

"Damn, they are a family of criminals! And I thought we were dealing with two brothers. Cross reference her name with 'Sebastian Daniels' and see what you produce," Naomi told Anthony.

"I was able to get the two files Margaret sent you unsealed as well," Taylor told Naomi.

Naomi read the files silently as she shook her head in disbelief. The pieces were falling into place as she continued to read. Despite the twisted details they uncovered, it was all making sense now. She printed copies of the new documents, adding them to the existing case folder. Taylor accompanied Naomi to the police station to meet Lieutenant Augustine. As they met in his office for a briefing, Naomi handed him a copy of the new documents. He flipped through each page slowly and then he sat straight up in his chair as if hit by an invisible electric charge. He immediately called to have the female suspect brought to one of the interrogation rooms and the male suspect in another.

"Let me handle the male suspect," Lieutenant Armstong said.

"Agreed," Naomi nodded.

"And when they bring her in, I'll get started on her and then I will let you take over," Lieutenant Augustine said.

"Sounds like a plan. I will follow your lead," Naomi agreed.

Lieutenant Augustine and Naomi entered the first dimly lit interrogation room, the air thick with tension. The male suspect sat in a metal chair, hands cuffed behind his back. Lieutenant Augustine did not waste any time.

"We know you were involved in the extortion scheme. Your sister has already given her side of the story. It's in your best interest to come clean," he said.

The brother smirked, leaning back in his chair, "My sister? She's got nothing to do with this, and if she said she did you forced her to lie," he told Lieutenant Augustine.

"Thanks for confirming your identity, jackass!" Naomi chimed in.

"We have evidence linking you to this crime scene and others," Augustine told him.

The brother's smirk faded as he leaned forward, his eyes narrowing. "I am not talking anymore. I want a lawyer."

With that request their interview was over. Naomi and Lieutenant Augustine retreated to the next interrogation room. Across the table sat their next suspect with a defiant glare, her hands cuffed in front of her.

Lieutenant Augustine began, his voice steady, "Do you know why you're here? We have evidence linking you to the hotel crime scene."

She tossed her dark hair over her shoulder and snorted. "Evidence? Please, you have nothing on me," she scoffed. She was taught to be hard.

Lieutenant Augustine leaned forward, his eyes locked on hers.

"Your brother is already talking to one of our detectives. It's only a matter of time before—"

"Before what?" She interrupted, her voice rising. "You think you can scare me into confessing? I'm not some rookie you can intimidate," she said smugly.

The Lieutenant sighed, pulling out a folder and sliding it across the table. "We have surveillance footage, witness statements, and more. Cooperate, and maybe the DA will consider leniency," he told her.

Her eyes flickered to the folder, then back to Augustine. She leaned back in her chair, crossing her arms.

"You need me to unravel this whole mess, don't you? Without me, you've got a puzzle with missing pieces," she smiled.

"Actually, we don't need you, Megan. Megan Young or do you prefer Megan Jeffrey," Naomi said, sliding documents from the folder one by one. She pulled out her photo, then fingerprints and a birth certificate.

Megan's eyes widened with fear now. Lieutenant Augustine looked on proudly.

"And Morgan is your twin brother, and we have him right next door giving his statement. Maurice must be the brother that we are searching for, but I do have one question—which of you killed Mason? Or should I say Sebastian?" Naomi asked, watching Megan squirm.

The juvenile records Taylor was able to have unsealed provided them with more in-depth details of the Jeffrey family which consisted of their parents, Sebastian, and Natalie Jeffrey, along with their four children, Maurice the eldest, Mason, then twins Megan and Morgan. Their parents divorced when the children were young, Maurice was fifteen at the time. Sebastian began drinking heavily once his wife left him and the children behind. He was tragically killed in a car accident and the children went into the foster care system. The twins who were seven years old were adopted within a month but Maurice and Mason, eleven years old, stayed in the system.

"We are offering you one chance to make a deal and help yourself Megan. You will not be able to survive going to prison for murder," Naomi said, sliding a picture of Mason Jeffrey's body towards her.

Megan looked at the picture and began sobbing uncontrollably. She knew something had happened but did not know what. That hard façade faded away as she tried to compose herself.

"I'll tell you whatever you want," she said, defeated.

"Where's Maurice?" Naomi asked.

"I never thought he would kill Mason," she said softly.

"What happened Megan?" Naomi asked.

"We were young when our father died, and our family was separated. Morgan and I had a good life for 10 years until Maurice found us. He wanted to reconnect the family, and we were happy to see him at first. He told us since our father died he was the man of the family, and it was his job to take care of us, not strangers. Mason had gotten caught up with drugs and he used that to get close to us. He helped Mason get straight and Mason appreciated his big brother taking care of him, we all did. But Maurice had a dark side. He hated our mother for leaving us and held her responsible for our father's death."

"We started out with robbing rich woman of their jewelry, but after 5 years he wasn't satisfied with that any longer, so he started this crazy scheme. He wanted to embarrass and humiliate the women instead, each time hoping to get back at our mother," Megan hung her head recounting what they did.

"And how did you pick the women?" Lieutenant Augustine chimed in.

"Maurice would pay off a maid or hotel staff to get in the rooms to search their belongings. He even paid someone at the registration desk to get a list of guests for the convention. He used the name 'Sebastian Daniels' for everything when he checked in at the hotels or registered at the conventions. Sebastian was our father's name," she told them.

"We need the names of those that helped him," Lieutenant Augustine said.

"I don't know all their names, but Morgan may know, and Mason worked with Maurice closer than any of us," she said.

"What happened to Mason?" Naomi asked.

"One of the women Mason was dealing with woke up and we almost got caught and she refused to pay. Then he felt sorry for this other lady when he found out she had a son. Maurice set up a meeting with the lady to get her money, but Mason was trying to get to her first to tell her what happened, then Maurice found out and he was furious. He would not tell us what he did, but I knew when Mason didn't come back home something bad happened. Maurice just said Mason wouldn't work the game anymore," Megan recounted.

"Where is Maurice?" Naomi asked her again.

"I honestly don't know. We always meet back at a designated location and if we all don't show up within twenty-four hours it's assumed something didn't go right and we go our separate ways until Maurice contacts us," she said.

"We need that location," Lieutenant Augustine said, handing her a pen and paper.

"What's going to happen to Morgan?" She asked as she wrote the information he requested.

"If he is willing to corroborate your story and had no involvement in your brother's murder, we will see what we can do," Lieutenant Augustine told her.

"Can I see Morgan so he can hear it from me about Mason," she asked in a whisper.

"Not at this time, but we will need to get you processed first then you can see him," Lieutenant Augustine explained.

Lieutenant Augustine called for an officer to bring Megan Jeffrey back to the booking area. The officer led her away in handcuffs as she looked back toward Naomi and Lieutenant Augustine, "For what it's worth, I am sorry," Megan said softly.

Uniformed officers led Megan and Morgan down a small hallway. They briefly made eye contact, and he could see his sister had been crying, realizing now he had failed to protect her as he promised he would always do. They arrived at a small room, its walls adorned with charts and a large ink pad resting on a metal table. Officer Louis, a seasoned police officer with a no-nonsense demeanor, stood ready, a stack of fingerprint cards by his side.

"Next," he barked, causing Megan to jump.

The officer uncuffed Megan and stepped back as Officer Louis took over. He grabbed Megan's left hand firmly, pressing each finger onto the ink pad then rolling it onto the card, leaving behind a trail of black smudges – the unique signature of Megan's identity. She was then escorted to have her mugshot photographed. Morgan followed after her, repeating the same procedure. They were both escorted to another area where Lieutenant Augustine and Naomi were waiting. As promised, the siblings were allowed to speak to one another briefly.

"Morgan, Maurice killed Mason," she whispered.

"Did those cops lie to you to get you to talk?" He asked.

"No, they showed me the pictures of his body, he's really dead. Maurice lied to us. He killed our brother and just left him like trash," she cried.

Morgan could not comfort his sister since their hands were cuffed. He tried to contain his anger.

"What do I need to do?" Morgan asked Lieutenant Augustine.

"Do you rescind your right to counsel?" He asked him.

"Yes, I do," Morgan said emphatically.

"We need your statement in writing," the Lieutenant said.

Morgan agreed on one condition, he asked if they could be uncuffed for a minute so he could console his sister. The minute seemed like an eternity to them, but it was just what they both needed. Their family now consisted only of shattered dreams.

Both siblings were charged and escorted to separate holding cells until their arraignment.

"Naomi, I must commend you for your detailed work in solving this case, but we still have to find Maurice Jeffrey. I will send officers to check out this address," he said, pointing to the paper Megan wrote on.

"My team is on it too, we are looking into an IP address he sent an email from to get a location on him," Naomi shared.

Chapter 14

Anthony sat quietly in the dim glow of his laptop screen, the only source of light in the otherwise darkened hotel room of their surveillance suite. The clock ticked past midnight, but the hour did nothing to inhibit his determination. He had been chasing down every lead they came across, but he felt the breakthrough was within reach.

The suspect, known now as Maurice Jeffrey had been careful, always one step ahead. But he made a mistake; he sent an email without routing it through another network. It was a small slip, a momentary lapse that left a digital fingerprint—an IP address.

Anthony's fingers bopped across the keyboard as he entered the IP address into his latest tracking software. The code ran, lines of text scrolling past faster than the eye could follow. Then, it stopped. The address was traced back to an old warehouse in a popular area of San Diego. Anthony called Naomi who was eagerly waiting for his call.

"Naomi, I've got a location. 55 Hempfield Drive. It's him. I'm sure of it," Anthony confirmed.

Naomi jumped out of bed, on high alert.

"Taylor, Anthony tracked him down!" She said pushing him, forcing him to get up.

Naomi called Lieutenant Augustine to let him know they now had a location and gave him the address.

"Can my team join you for his capture? We will stay clear of any police activity," Naomi said.

After a brief silence he agreed knowing the police would not have gotten this far without Naomi's agency.

"Your team can be onsite, but everyone will need to stay in the vehicle at all times," he told her.

"Agreed," Naomi said.

Naomi and her team prepared to leave to meet the police at their designated spot.

"Anthony, bring your equipment so we can capture as much as possible from the car," Naomi said, with determination in her voice.

The police assembled quickly, a symphony of silent proficiency. The night air was thick with tension as the San Diego Police Department surrounded the nondescript warehouse on the edge of the Gaslamp Quarter. Lieutenant Augustine gave the signal, and they breached, bursting through the front entry with a force that shattered the silence of the night. Inside, they found their suspect, a man in his mid-thirties, sitting alone in a makeshift command center, as the police approached, they triggered a trip wire that activated a smoke canister, as the leader of the city's most notorious extortion ring, Maurice Jeffrey orchestrated his escape.

Naomi sat in the car with her team, her eyes fixed on the building's rear exit. She knew Maurice was desperate and dangerous, but she was determined to bring him to justice.

Suddenly, a loud bang echoed through the alleyways, and a figure dashed from the warehouse's back door. It was Maurice, clutching a duffel bag presumably filled with money and stolen goods. Naomi sprang into action, jumping from the car, her footsteps pounding the pavement as she gave chase.

"Naomi!" Taylor shouted, running behind her, adrenaline pumping through his veins.

Maurice was agile, darting through the narrow streets with the familiarity of a man who had spent his life evading the law. But Naomi was relentless, her training and resolve pushing her forward. Taylor kept up with her stride for stride. The chase led them through the heart of the city, past the blinking lights of downtown, and into the labyrinth of the historic district.

As they neared the marina, Maurice made a daring leap onto an anchored boat. Naomi and Taylor followed behind him, her heart racing. The boat rocked violently under their weight, and for a moment, it seemed as if Maurice would slip away into the dark waters of the bay. But Taylor was too quick. He tackled him just as he was about to start the engine, and they both tumbled to the deck. Maurice fought fiercely, but Taylor's grip was like a vice. With a swift move, he subdued him until the police arrived to take Maurice into custody, the sound of the metal handcuffs clicking shut echoing in the night. As Naomi caught her breath, she looked out at the city skyline. The chase was over, she could bring closure to all his victims.

"Naomi, what were you thinking chasing after a killer?" Taylor said, still catching his breath.

"I just could not let him get away," Naomi responded, defending her actions.

"You're determined to drive me crazy, lady," he said, reaching out for her hand.

"I knew you would follow me," Naomi smiled.

"Just like you chased after your purse snatcher when we first met, you couldn't let him get away either," Taylor laughed.

"We would not have met had I not," Naomi winked.

Naomi and Taylor returned to their van to let the rest of the team in on the capture of Jeffrey.

San Diego police completed the search of Maurice Jeffrey's hideout and was able to secure solid evidence along with names of his accomplices. Lieutenant Augustine planned to file arrest warrants for all involved. The next day they were able to arrest four additional suspects.

As Naomi and her team packed their belongings Naomi contacted Sergeant McLaughlin

"Sergeant, it's Naomi. I've got great news about the Collins case," she said.

"Don't leave me hanging, Naomi," Sergeant McLaughlin said.

"We got him. Your murder suspect was apprehended last night in San Diego," she shared.

"Good work, Naomi. I owe you one," he told her.

"Just doing my job, Sergeant. I'll have Lieutenant Augustine send over the arrest report and evidence files," she said.

"Did you tell him how you chased down a dangerous murderer," Taylor interrupted.

"Was that Mr. Sylvester? What did he say?" Sergeant McLaughlin inquired.

"Nothing sir, we will talk later," Naomi told him, shaking her head at Taylor.

"All facts," Taylor said. "Can't argue with facts ma'am."

Naomi sat at the desk in the hotel suite to call Cassandra with the good news. With phone in hand, Naomi rehearsed the words she was about to deliver. She dialed the number of her friend Cassandra. The phone rang twice before a cautious voice answered, "Hello?"

"Cassandra, it's Naomi," she said, her tone a blend of professionalism and reassurance. "I have wonderful news."

There was a pause, a breath held in anticipation. "Yes?" Cassandra wondered.

"The individual who's been blackmailing you is now in police custody," Naomi declared, allowing the weight of her words to sink in.

A gasp escaped Cassandra's lips, followed by a nervous, "How? When?"

"Last night," Naomi explained. "We caught him red-handed with the evidence. The police have everything they need to keep him behind bars for a long time."

Tears of relief and gratitude mingled in Cassandra's voice. "I... I don't know how to thank you, Naomi. You've given me my life back."

Naomi smiled faintly, a sense of accomplishment warming her up.

"Just doing my job, Cassandra. But remember, this is just the beginning. We'll need your statement to make the charges stick," Naomi told her.

"I'll do whatever it takes," Cassandra affirmed, her voice now steady with resolve.

"Good. I'll be home tomorrow to go over everything. For now, rest easy knowing he can't harm you anymore."

As they said their goodbyes, Naomi hung up the phone and leaned back in her chair. Justice had been served, and for the first time in a long while, she felt a surge of victory coursing through her.

Their three- and half-hour flight back to New Orleans was uneventful, Naomi slept most of the way home. The humid air of New Orleans wrapped around Naomi and her team like a familiar shawl as they stepped off the plane. The scent of magnolias and the distant sound of jazz were a stark contrast to the dry, pulsing heat of San Diego they had left behind.

Naomi's heart drummed with a mixture of relief and anticipation. The undercover operation had been grueling, but they had gathered the evidence needed to dismantle an extensive extortion ring. Now, back on her home turf, she felt the weight of her false identity melting away.

"Feels good to be back, doesn't it?" Taylor said, collecting their bags.

"Better than good," Naomi replied, her eyes scanning the crowd. "It feels right."

The team made their way to the exit, their steps almost in sync, a silent rhythm honed by weeks of working undercover. As they approached the airport exit, a surprise awaited them. Naomi spotted a welcome party consisting of Maragret Regis, Cassandra, and her husband along with Brian, holding her French bulldog, Saint, who was wriggling with excitement.

Naomi's professional demeanor cracked, a smile breaking through as Saint ran towards her, sliding across the floor with eagerness. Laughter erupted from the group as she knelt down, embracing the chaos of fur.

"Missed you too, buddy," she whispered into Saint's ear, her voice thick with emotion.

The reunion was short but sweet. There was work to be done, and the team was eager to start. They said their goodbyes, promising to catch up properly once the case was officially closed.

Back at the agency, the team huddled around the evidence board. Photos, notes, and strings creating a web of connections that only they could untangle. Naomi felt a surge of pride. They were close to bringing justice to all the victims. The only thing left was the trial. Naomi gathered all of the evidence they collected and gave it to Margaret Regis so she could make copies and send them off to both Dallas and San Diego police departments.

Three months later the courtroom in San Diego was a frenzy of hushed whispers and shuffling papers as the spectators awaited the next phase of the trial. The defendant, Maurice Jeffrey, sat stoically, his eyes betraying nothing of the turmoil that might be churning within. He was known in the darker corners of the city as a ruthless extortionist, but today, he was simply a man facing the ugly truth of his crime. This was the first of his trials.

The prosecutor rose, her voice clear and resonant. "The court will now hear the testimony of the defendant's family," she announced, and a collective breath seemed to be drawn in by the room.

First to take the stand was Jeffrey's younger sister, Megan. Her hands trembled, not with fear, but with the weight of the truth she was about to unveil.

"My brother," she began, her voice a mere whisper, "was once the kindest soul you could ever meet at first. But revenge and hate... it twisted him into someone we no longer recognized."

She recounted tales of intimidation, the schemes he orchestrated and had his siblings carry out, of the coldness that had settled in her brother's heart.

"I still care about him, but I cannot hide what he has become, nor how we hurt other people," she concluded, a solitary tear trailing down her cheek.

The courtroom sat in stunned silence as Jeffrey's mother, a tall, sophisticated looking woman walked forward, taking a seat on the witness stand.

"I tried to shield my children from the ugly truth about their father. He was a cruel and abusive man. When I found out about the illegal business dealings, I tried to take my children, but he threatened to hunt us down and kill us. I had no choice but to leave. He poisoned their heads with lies about me. I should have been stronger and gone to the police, but now I see it only created a monster," she said, her voice heavy with sorrow. "It breaks my heart to see the path he chose."

As the family's testimonies wove a narrative of downfall and regret, Jeffrey's fierce facade began to crack. For the first time, there was a glimpse of the boy he used to be, the boy his family mourned for. The final blow came from Jeffrey's brother Morgan, who knew all the details of Maurice's extortion scheme. He had taken a deal the police offered a few months back by disclosing where documents were kept and the location of the money and stolen property.

"Maurice took advantage of me, and my twin sister Megan and I am here today to stand up for what's right," he said, standing tall and resolute. "To stand up against the fear he caused."

His words hung in the air, a poignant echo of the justice that was to come. As he stepped down, the jury's gaze followed him, their minds made up.

The trial continued, but the verdict was written on the faces of the family of Maurice Jeffrey, the extortionist who had gripped the city in fear.

The jury came back in under an hour with a guilty verdict. Maurice was immediately taken into custody and would be extradited to stand trial in

Dallas. The twins, Megan, and Morgan Jeffrey each received a 5-year sentence for their part in the extortion scheme along with a $25,000 fine.

The office of the **Secure Justice Agency** was alive with an electric buzz, a stark contrast to its usual hushed tones of secrecy and discretion. The last rays of the setting sun filtered through the blinds, casting glow over the celebratory scene. The faint sounds of jazz trumpets in the background aided in the festivities. At the center of the room stood Naomi, all smiles, her eyes sparkling with triumph. She raised her champagne glass, the light catching the bubbles as they danced to the top.

"To the team," she toasted, her voice steady but filled with emotion, "who worked tirelessly to crack Cassandra's case."

The team erupted into cheers, the jovial sound mingling with the clink of glasses. Balloons bobbled against the ceiling, and a banner reading 'Case Closed!' hung proudly above the doorway. The room was filled with the agency's staff, from the seasoned investigators to the eager interns, all sharing in the moment of victory.

Cassandra and her family were present as well.

Cassandra stepped forward with tears of joy in her eyes, "You all have given me my life back."

Taylor and Charles shook hands, sealing the bond the two had forged.

"I am forever in your debt," Charles told Taylor.

"What are your plans Cassandra, now that this is all behind you?" Naomi asked.

"Charles and I talked about taking a long trip to heal and reconnect as family," Cassandra shared.

Anthony grinned from behind his laptop, where a complex network of data had finally yielded the breakthrough they needed. "Couldn't have done it without your genius, Anthony," Naomi acknowledged with a nod in his direction.

"It was truly a team effort," Taylor said, proud of how hard the team worked.

Laughter and chatter filled the room as anecdotes from the case were shared. Cassandra's case had been a labyrinth of puzzles and dead ends, but together, they had navigated its twists and turns to deliver justice. As the evening wore on, the team gathered around the large oak table, laden with an assortment of finger foods, desserts, and more bottles of champagne. They recounted the moments of doubt, the breakthroughs, and the final, exhilarating rush as the pieces fell into place. And to top it off, their fearless leader chased down the suspect. Joseph even gifted her with a pair of running shoes as a joke.

Naomi looked around at her team, her family in arms, and felt a surge of pride. They were more than just investigators; they were guardians of truth in a world that often seemed wrapped in shadows. The celebration continued into the night, a well-deserved respite from the rigors of their profession. For tonight, they were not just the parts in the wheel of justice—they were its champions.

The last echoes of celebration had faded from the walls of the **Secure Justice Agency**, leaving behind a silence that was almost tangible. Naomi sat at her desk, the glow of the desk lamp casting a warm halo in the dim room. The case that had consumed her time for the past few months was now closed, its complexities unraveled by her unyielding determination.

The files on her desk were neatly stacked, each one a testament to the tangled journey she had undertaken. The case that had started with her trying to clear her friend of murder, spiraled into a web of deceit involving wealthy women and a broken, estranged family.

Naomi leaned back in her chair, her mind replaying the pivotal moments that led to the case's resolution. It was her keen eye for detail that had noticed there was more than one perpetrator, her intuition that had sensed the link between the seemingly unrelated events, and her courage that had confronted the mastermind in the final act of this real-life drama. The agency's team had been indispensable. Each member had brought their unique skills to the table, from Oliver and Joseph's tech wizardry to Anthony's undercover finesse. Together, they had formed an unbreakable chain that pulled through the murkiest depths of the case.

Now, with the accolades received and the client's gratitude expressed, Naomi felt a rare moment of peace. The thrill of the chase was intoxicating, but the quiet satisfaction of justice served was a feeling she cherished deeply.

The office door creaked open, and Taylor stepped in. "All set for the next adventure?" he asked, a smile in his voice.

Naomi looked up, her eyes reflecting a spark of the fire that made her the best in her field. "Only if you go with me," she replied, her voice steady and sure. "Then I definitely am."

Taylor nodded and closed the door behind him, it was them against the world. Naomi took a moment to savor the stillness and his soothing presence. **Secure Justice Detective Agency** had once again lived up to its name, and as its leader, she had steered them through the storm. But the world outside was never still for long, and Naomi would always be ready to answer the call. Naomi and Taylor headed to the elevator, the doors opened, and a man stumbled out, collapsing at their feet.

"Naomi," he mumbled.

"Who is this man, Naomi?" Taylor wondered.

"Oh, my goodness, it's Theodore Miller, call 911," Naomi screamed.

This was the beginning of another case to investigate.

About the Author

Born and raised in New Orleans, LA. She is a wife and mother of three daughters. Dr. Sybil H. Taylor is a clinical pharmacist, author, and entrepreneur. Dr. Taylor earned a Bachelor of Science degree in pharmacy and a doctorate and clinical pharmacy. Dr. Taylor has worked in various pharmacy settings, including retail, institutional hospital, and federal government. Dr. Taylor first published Friendly Betrayal in December 2001. In August 2005, hurricane Katrina destroyed all printed and digital copies of her original novel. Dr. Taylor has since relocated to Atlanta, Georgia raised three children and started her own natural skincare business, Scripted Naturals in February 2020. Dr. Taylor was fortunate to locate a copy of her original novel to republish as she returns to writing, one of her many passions.

Read more at https://www.scriptednaturals.com.

www.ingramcontent.com/pod-product-compliance
Lightning Source LLC
Chambersburg PA
CBHW050409030726
47503CB00006B/2100